CITIZENS OF LIGHT

CITIZENS OF LIGHT

A Novel

Sam Shelstad

BRINDLE
AND GLASS

Edited by Claire Philipson
Proofread by Senica Maltese
Interior design by Sydney Barnes
Cover design by Ingrid Paulson

CATALOGUING DATA AVAILABLE FROM LIBRARY AND ARCHIVES CANADA
ISBN 9781990071058 (softcover)
ISBN 9781990071065 (electronic)

TouchWood Editions acknowledges that the land on which we live and work is
within the traditional territories of the Lkwungen (Esquimalt and Songhees),
Malahat, Pacheedaht, Scia'new, T'Sou-ke and W̱SÁNEĆ (Pauquachin, Tsartlip,
Tsawout, Tseycum) peoples.

We acknowledge the financial support of the Government of Canada through
the Canada Book Fund and the Canada Council for the Arts, and of the Province
of British Columbia through the British Columbia Arts Council and the Book
Publishing Tax Credit.

This book was printed using FSC®-certified, acid-free papers, processed chlorine
free, and printed with soya-based inks.

Printed in Canada

26 25 24 23 22 1 2 3 4 5

I had this Nevada woman on the line, and I could tell she was in it for the long haul. A tedious forty-five-minute electric company survey. Longer if the respondent was chatty. And that's all fine. That was my job, phoning people and conducting what could sometimes be forty-five-minute electric company surveys. The call centre had a rule though, where if your shift ended during a call you couldn't hang up until the survey was completed. My shift ended in five minutes and here was this lady, ready to go. I needed to get home. My mother had locked herself in the bathroom before I left for work. When something upsets her, she hides like a sick cat. She doesn't want to bother anyone, so she hides and ends up bothering everyone worse than if she'd only admitted she was upset. I called her on my break—no answer.

"How long is this gonna take, miss?" the Nevada woman said.

"Approximately forty-five minutes, depending on your answers," I said. This was where they usually hung up.

"Oh, good Lord. I'm watching my shows. Let's just get on with it."

"I can call back at a more convenient time." You could get written up for saying this if a supervisor was listening in, but I took a chance. If she hung up, I could still run and catch the 11:10 bus home.

"No, no. Just get on with your questions."

"Okay, great. Now before we start, I have to inform you that this call may be monitored for quality assurance and that—"

"What's your name again?" the woman said. "Karen?"

"Colleen Weagle." We were allowed to use pseudonyms. Mine was Annie Hart, but I felt bad about lying and just told everyone my real name.

"Colleen Weagle. Where are you calling from? Australia or something? You have a funny accent."

"I'm actually calling from Toronto, Canada."

"Canada? My brother has a friend up there. They met online. What's his name? Peter, I think. Peter Frost. My brother's always going on about Peter Frost. You wouldn't believe it. He lives in French Canada."

"Ma'am, just before we start, I have to inform you that this call may be monitored—"

"You said this already, get to your questions."

"Yes, well, I have to inform you—"

"Peter Frost runs a sports memorabilia shop up there. That's how my brother got involved with Peter. He collects baseball memorabilia."

We eventually got to the woman from Nevada's utility opinions. She would go off on some tangent and then, sensing my frustration, answer a few questions to keep me satisfied. I'd already packed up my *Riders of Exley* script—I usually chipped away at my TV specs while making calls—so I pulled the free *Metro* newspaper out of the recycling bin behind my desk. I hadn't finished the crossword that night, and thought I'd knock that out while the woman slogged through the survey.

I was flipping through the paper, getting to the puzzles, ushering the Nevada woman along as best I could, when I came across a photograph. I was struck. Two cops leading a criminal out of a casino. It wasn't the criminal that caught my attention though. Wasn't the cops either. It was a man in the background, wearing a vest. A Fallsview Casino employee. I knew him from somewhere.

"How satisfied are you with the *delivery* of your electric service?" I read from my computer screen. Then I shot my eyes back down to the *Metro*. There was something about that man in the vest. I had this feeling in my intestines. "Are you very satisfied, mostly satisfied, neither satisfied nor dissatisfied, mostly dissatisfied, or very dissatisfied?"

"Neither satisfied," the Nevada woman said. "I mean, it's electricity. They deliver it. What do you want from me? Hey, what's the weather like up there?"

"It's raining." It really was pouring. I could hear the rain smacking the windows over my headset—it sounded like the call centre was lurching through a car wash. I didn't have my umbrella. I'd have to use my newspaper to stay dry.

"Raining? How about that. It's not raining here at all. What time is it there?"

"It's 11:25."

"PM?"

"PM."

"How about that. How about that."

I burned a hole through the *Metro* paper with my eyes. My supervisor, Ken, burned a hole through me. I was the only dialer left and he couldn't pack up until I finished. I gave him one of those friendly shrugs to say, "Yes, I'm on your side, I wanna go home too." He looked away. Almost midnight. Still raining. The Nevada woman had ten questions left, but she put me on hold to feed her dachshunds. I stared at the man in the Fallsview vest.

While I waited for the woman to return to the phone, it hit me. Leonard's funeral. Three months earlier, my husband had passed away and the man in the vest was at the funeral. No one knew who he was or how he knew Leonard. I sure didn't know him. He stood in the back and didn't speak to anyone. I approached him after the service, thanked him for coming, and asked him how he knew Leonard. He said they'd worked together at the plastics plant. Then he immediately excused himself and left. Disappeared.

It was him alright. The wide face. The thin, long nose. Little predator eyes—he had this look. The photo wasn't all that clear and the man in the vest stood in the background, but it was clear enough.

"How much longer is this gonna take?" the Nevada woman said, picking up her phone. "Buck'll be home soon."

"There are ten questions left, ma'am. I can try and go faster."

"Please do. I don't have all day. How much are they paying you for this anyway? You know, my brother used to work at one of those phone places. I think he was selling cable subscriptions. Of course, Buck and I have satellite."

I looked over at Ken. He was doing angry stretching exercises in his cubicle. No headphones—he wasn't listening in.

I dropped the call.

I hung up my headset, signed off of my computer. Carefully tore the page with the photo from the *Metro*, then carefully tore the photo from the page. I placed the photo in my TV script notebook, which went back in my bag. Hanging up on a respondent mid-survey is a serious infraction, but I figured I was in the clear. Ken was the only supervisor there and he wasn't listening. I had to get out of there. It wasn't just that I had to get home to Mother. Sure, I was worried about her. When she locks herself in the bathroom, you can bet you're in for a long night. But the Nevada woman had been nearing the end of the survey—Mother could've waited ten or twenty minutes longer. No, what threw me was the man in the vest. He was at Leonard's funeral. It was him in the picture. I *knew* it was him. I couldn't concentrate on the call.

Me and Leonard were together for almost three years. He was my best friend, except for my mom. Kind and gentle. Always saying complimentary things about people when you brought them up in conversation. And thoughtful—not only did he buy me flowers on Valentine's Day but he'd buy them for Mother, too. That kind of man. And then out of nowhere, while I was asleep, three months earlier, I got a call. I thought Leonard was in the bed with me. He wasn't. He was in Morrison Bog. Almost a two hours' drive. A woman found him while walking her dog. Wearing black clothes, lying face first in the mud. Dead. Gunshot through the head. Self-inflicted, the cops declared.

It made zero sense. Leonard never went anywhere. He had no business in a bog. He was happy. Super positive about the world. And why was he wearing black clothes, like some cat burglar? No letter of explanation. His father's old hunting rifle. The police basically shrugged. His car was parked on a service road a few kilometres from where they found him. He'd driven out there, in the middle of the night, and then what? Ran into the forest and pulled the trigger on himself? It was like he had this secret life. His friends from the plastics plant were all dumbfounded too. It was devastating. Hard enough that Leonard was gone. Not knowing why, not being able to ask him what had happened? I couldn't take it. But I had to take it, so I did.

After meeting that man at the funeral, the man from the *Metro* photograph, I thought maybe he knew something. He seemed nervous when I talked to him, and he didn't appear to be acquainted with anybody else. I was curious, so I asked around and no one among the small crowd gathered at the funeral knew him. Including Leonard's coworkers. Leonard's boss from Conter Plastics was in attendance and said he'd never seen the guy. The man had lied to me about working at the plant with Leonard. I knew then that this stranger might have some connection to my late husband's driving out to Morrison Bog. To his death. He might even be responsible for it, I thought. I called the police, told them about the suspicious man at the funeral. They told me to get more sleep. I never saw the stranger again and his troubling presence was left to bounce around in my brain with the rest of the upsetting details surrounding Leonard's death. Another layer of grief tossed upon the pile.

But now I had the photograph. I knew where the man lived, or at least where he worked. Fallsview Casino in Niagara Falls. I wasn't sure what to do with this information, but I knew I had to leave.

2

"Colleen," a voice said. I stood at the punch-in clock, looking for my card so I could swipe out. I turned around.

Patti Houlihan. Most of my co-workers were teenagers, but Patti was in her late thirties, like me. She lived in Mimico, where I lived.

Patti could win a beauty contest if she wasn't always scowling. She has shiny black hair like Monica from *Friends* and perfect posture. Cartoonish eyes, like dinner plates. In a good way. Big brown eyes. Adorable freckles dusted across her cheeks. But then that scowl works against all those nice features.

Me, I try to smile as much as possible. I'm not much to look at with a neutral expression, but I'm proud of my smile and I wear it generously. A good smile increases your attractiveness tenfold. I have stringy brown hair that I dye blond every two months. Pressed-in raisin-like eyes with wrinkles. The figure of a skinny teenage boy—the slumped posture, too. Patti has curves and turns heads and all that, but I'm not jealous. I make sure to smile, and it's a genuine smile. People respond to that. It's true.

"Hi, Patti," I said. "You got stuck too, huh? I thought everyone left."

"Oh, so you were stuck on a survey, were you? Thought everyone left? What a coincidence."

"Pardon me?"

"It's raining, Colleen. Don't be such a sneak. You could have just asked me for a ride."

"No, I—"

"Don't worry about it. It's fine. I'll give you a goddamn ride. You don't have to be all sneaky and lie about being on a survey, is all I'm saying. Hurry up though. I'm not waiting around."

"No, I'm ready."

I found my card, swiped out, then Patti did the same. I followed her to the elevator. Most nights, we'd both finish our shifts at eleven and Patti would offer me a ride home. Usually, I'd try and duck her. I didn't feel like listening to her rants after being on the phone for six hours and the bus ride offered me a chance to decompress before I had to deal with Mother. That night was no exception—while I was eager to get home, I hadn't had the chance to process what I'd seen in the *Metro*. The mystery man had resurfaced. Fallsview Casino. This was huge, but with Patti and then my mother, it would be hours before I could collect my thoughts. And you couldn't refuse a ride from Patti Houlihan. She'd take offense. One time I tried passing up her offer and she threw my backpack into the street.

The rain was still coming down hard. Patti didn't offer to share her umbrella, so I held my bag above my head. Hopefully my spec scripts will stay dry, I thought. The *Metro* photograph, too. I didn't want to have to track down another copy. Patti had parked on the street two blocks away.

"Slow down," Patti said. She strolled along casually, as if she was meandering through a museum. "You're being rude. I'm driving you home."

"Sorry," I said, walking back to her side. I was getting soaked. "It's just cold."

"Should have brought your umbrella. God, Colleen. *I* thought to bring an umbrella. The problem with you is you don't think. Speaking of which, do we need to stop at an ATM?"

"Sorry, yes. Unless I can pay you tomorrow?"

"Fat chance. If you can't remember your umbrella when the forecast says rain, you won't remember my money. I'll stop at the Sunoco and you can run in. But be quick. I'm not missing James Corden."

Patti charged me ten dollars a ride. A taxi from the office to Mimico would cost twenty, Patti argued. Plus tip. Public transit might be cheaper, she said, but then I'd be waiting around in the dark for buses and stopping at all the stops and who knows what could happen on those deathtraps. The ten bucks wasn't just for gas. Patti had car payments, insurance, etc. If anything, she felt, I was taking advantage of her. This seemed a bit off to me, but I had no counter-argument.

We drove home to Mimico. Patti went on about her day, gave me a detailed rundown of each call she'd made, reflected on the rampant stupidity of the general population, and explained how the call centre was entirely beneath her station. She'd worked there for nearly a decade. I didn't say anything. Rain pelted the roof of her Sunbird. We stopped at the Sunoco so I could withdraw her fare from the ATM. I came out with Patti's money and the passenger door was locked. She rolled down the window.

"I'm gonna leave you here," she said, reaching for her money. "I don't wanna miss Corden. Anyway, it's a five-minute walk from here. You'll be fine."

She left.

I removed my backpack, held it above my head, and started walking home.

I grew up in Mimico, which is in South Etobicoke, which is part of Toronto. It feels like its own little town. Toronto is like that—a series of villages all smushed together. When I went to college, I briefly lived in an apartment downtown with two roommates. I spent eight months on a farm a few hours west of Toronto as a teenager. Otherwise, I've spent my entire life in the same small bedroom in Mother's corn-yellow bungalow. We live on a quiet street, but our backyard shares a fence with The Blue Drop, a sports bar. It was a jazz club when I was little—the new owners kept the name, changed everything else. I've seen people having sex up against the dumpster from my bedroom window. The noise was never that bad though. A nice neighbourhood. Mostly older Italians and yuppies. The prettiest dogs you've ever seen. I didn't need to get a dog myself and waste money on the big bags of food, because I could step outside and watch them all parade past.

I stepped inside the house, my jeans and new Gap hoodie heavy with water. I peeled everything off, dropped it all on the floor, called out to Mother in my underwear. No answer. I wiped myself dry with one of Leonard's scarves, still hanging in the entranceway, and walked into the living room. Mother was sitting on the couch. Her head hanging over the back of the couch, mouth agape. It looked like she was dead. The TV was on, but it was the settings menu.

"Mother!" I said.

She opened her eyes and coughed.

"What time is it?" she asked. She sat up and cracked her neck.

"I don't know. It's late. What are you doing? Why didn't you answer the phone earlier? I called on my break."

"I'm so sorry, honey. Were you very worried? I ruined your night, didn't I?"

"I'm fine, Mother. Are *you* okay?"

"I was just tired. I'm tired."

"Well, I'm glad you're okay. You took your new medication?"

"I took my new medication."

"What did you do tonight?"

"Oh, nothing. You probably want to watch TV. I'll get out of your way. I was trying to increase the brightness, dear. I hope I didn't ruin the TV for you. Where are your clothes?"

"It's raining."

"Is it, now? I would've paid for your taxi."

"Well, I'm going to make a snack and go to my room. Do you want some toast?"

"No, no. You just go on."

In the kitchen, waiting for my toast to pop, I started putting away the dishes that were sitting in the drying rack. I was shivering—still in my underwear, still damp—but I wanted to get my snack and lock myself in my room before Mother started up again. You think you're in the clear when you catch her in a calm mood, but that can change in an instant. She'll enter the room and start in on some asinine issue—how the squirrels in the backyard seem like they're too tired, something like that—and before you know it, her eyes will well up. She'll apologize for some imagined offense, beg for forgiveness, and then run off to the basement. Squeeze herself between the washer and the dryer. Mother has carried around this strange guilt complex since my eight-month stint on the Citizens of Light Rejuvenation Farm when I was sixteen.

The Farm was a large and derelict country estate outside of Lucan, Ontario, run by a man named Father Woodbine. I was a different person before I ended up there. Troubled. Angry. Dropping acid at my friend Claire's house after school. Shoplifting from the Eaton Centre. One night the cops brought me home after I'd been caught hopping the fence at Christie Pits pool with my friends. They'd found a cassette tape case with two joints in it in my pocket. Mother threatened to kick me out and I called her bluff. I decided to run away. One of Woodbine's associates approached me at the Greyhound station as I scanned the departures board for inspiration. I would never have really left the city if he hadn't intervened. That's how Woodbine and his followers recruited new Citizens of Light—they found young runaways like me at bus stations or hitchhiking along the highway and enticed them into their world.

The associate who brought me in was attractive and kind. He listened to my story, exhibited compassion. Showed me pictures of The Farm, with beautiful fields, a pond, and a big, long table in the kitchen with people my age eating spaghetti together. So, I went with him. When I arrived at The Farm, everyone was so welcoming. I felt accepted, like I had real worth. The dark religious stuff was introduced gradually. It didn't really sink in that I was part of a cult until after the cops descended on the property eight months later and took us all away. Woodbine went to prison. I went back to Mimico with Mother and things changed. My rebellious phase had reached its conclusion. I stayed home on the weekends. I had to see a psychologist every Monday night. I went on medication to help me sleep. And Mother's guilt over what had happened to me slowly took over her life.

She had kept this condition somewhat under control after years of therapy, but lately it had been flaring up again. Since Leonard's passing. I felt for her, I really did. But it was exhausting. I had my own guilt. My own grief. I needed to be alone in my room, with the door shut against the world.

I was putting away the last dish, a blue mug, when I happened to read the block letters printed on the side: Niagara Falls. The Niagara Falls mug. I'd washed it a hundred times before. I'd drunk my coffee out of it fifty times, watched Leonard and Mother drink coffee out of it, too. It sat among the objects decorating my daily routines, but I'd never really noticed it before. Just a mug we happened to have.

But now, considering what I'd seen that night in the *Metro*, the mug took on new meaning. *Niagara Falls*. How did it get here? I didn't buy it. I'd never been to Niagara Falls. Neither had Mother, as far as I knew. Had Leonard? Or did his friend, the man in the vest, give it to him as a gift? Where did the damn thing come from?

I held the mug under the light and examined it. I'm not sure what I was looking for. It was a blue mug. But this much was clear:

Whatever secret life Leonard had going for himself, it had something to do with Niagara Falls. All signs pointed that way. The man in the photograph, the mug. Morrison Bog was only a half-hour drive from Niagara Falls. I had to go. I had to go as soon as possible. I worked Friday nights and Sunday afternoons, so weekends were out. I had Saturdays and Tuesdays off—a day trip wouldn't do though. I needed a weekend. Which meant I'd have to book a weekend off, and you have to do that at least two weeks in advance. I'd leave in two weeks. I'd go to Niagara Falls, I'd go to the Fallsview Casino, and I'd track down the man in the photograph. Then I'd find out what had happened to Leonard.

I went to my room so I could play my computer game. I brought the mug with me. I heard the toast pop on my way down the hall, but I just left it there.

3

Heartsong trotted along Lorenzo Snow Beach under the moon-light. Heading for Main Pool. Tiki torches burned a hazy yellow alongside the huts farther up the shore. No one else around—Heartsong had the beach to himself. Will Bonsai show up? I won-dered. Maybe he would be waiting by the pond.

Heartsong was Leonard's character in *Reindeer Island*, an online computer game he'd played endlessly. It took place on a luxury resort island with hotels, a rock spa, a wedding chapel—and no humans. Just reindeer, controlled by other online players. There were puzzles scattered around the island and they all re-quired at least two players to solve them. For example, if two reindeer each stood where certain symbols were marked on the ground at the same time, a secret cave would open. The catch was that you could only communicate through a few simple gestures, like stamping your left or right hoof. Or, if you ate a piece of fruit from one of the island's fruit trees, you could make your antlers glow the colour of the fruit. The challenge was supposed to be figuring out how to coordinate with other players and solve the puzzles without using traditional language, but the real difficulty was finding other players. It was rare to see other reindeer on the island, aside from Bonsai. Not a terribly popular game. All the buildings, clubs, and gardens on the island seemed to be named after Mormon prophets or angels, which I guess the game designer sneaked in there. Or maybe it had been developed by the Mormon church to spread word of their faith. Leonard wasn't religious but he liked running around on the island as a reindeer. He played every day. After he died, I discovered that he hadn't logged out of the game. I could play as his character, his reindeer. I felt close to him walking around as Heartsong. I was continuing his game. It was like part of Leonard was still alive inside *Reindeer Island*.

Exiting the beach, Heartsong took the stone bridle path up toward the Golden Plates Hotel. Crickets buzzed through the laptop speakers. A blue mist hung low on the ground.

Heartsong turned off the path when the Golden Plates parking lot came into view and went past the tennis courts. Slipping around the corner of the clubhouse, he stepped out onto the enormous deck of Main Pool. Starlight shimmered atop the water's surface. Poolside furniture lined up in perfect rows, empty. And there was the silver reindeer. His name, Bonsai, floated above him in a yellow font. Standing stock-still under the waterslide, he looked back at Heartsong.

Heartsong weaved through chairs and collapsed umbrellas. He walked up to Bonsai and stood before him on the pool deck. The two reindeer looked at each other. The player who controlled Bonsai was watching Heartsong on another screen. If a reindeer was left inactive for five minutes, they would fall asleep, and Bonsai was awake. Heartsong stamped twice with his right hoof. The silver reindeer disappeared—whoever was controlling him had logged out.

I hardly slept. Since Leonard died, I hardly slept anyway, but the *Metro* photograph made things worse. I wanted to take off the man's Fallsview vest and strangle him with it. Which isn't fair. I didn't know this man. He could be a saint. But he was also my only potential connection to the other world Leonard must have occupied, the one with late-night bog visits. And he seemed out of place at the funeral. He didn't talk to anyone, never offered his condolences. He'd lied about working at Conter Plastics. It was impossible not to regard him as sinister—especially at 2 AM, when I'm rolling around in bed, twisting up the sheets, eyes wide open.

At 6:29 AM, I watched my phone until the alarm came on. I turned it off before it buzzed. And then I got up and began my routines. Even if you're not happy with your life, a solid routine will keep you from being too mopey. There's no time to dwell on terrible things if you're on a tight schedule. When Leonard died, I took some time off from work and it was dark. Oh, the darkness. All I did was cry and have these fantasies that Leonard was alive and my thinking that he had died in the mud was a kind of psychosis. Sometimes I closed my eyes and imagined I was a bronze sculpture in a park that felt zero emotions and even withstood lightning strikes with indifference. The call centre had given me the whole month off, but I didn't want the month off. I wanted to make calls. I was back in my swivel chair, headset on, four days after Leonard's funeral.

I stayed focused. My number of completed surveys per hour actually went up. I worked on my TV scripts. I looked after Mother, as much as she would allow me to. I downloaded games onto my phone and played them until I couldn't progress any further. Completed every challenge on *Temple Run 2*. It was only at night, when I turned the lights off and lay down, with everything I could possibly do in a day already done, that the darkness crept back in. The crying, the fantasies. I'd squeeze my wrists and bite my pillow. But even these long nights weren't so terrible because I knew I could just wait them out, morning would eventually come, and I could start on my routine again.

I'm most creative in the morning, so I like to get going on my spec scripts straight away. Quick shower, brush my teeth, and then off to Piccolos to write. Piccolos is an Italian café in Mimico. They have tables out on the sidewalk, like in Europe. If you get there early, you can grab one of these tables and work away in the morning sun, inspired by the passersby and dog walkers and traffic. Sitting out there, working on my scripts feels like a mix of Los Angeles and Paris. Two places I've never been—but you get the gist from TV and the internet.

When I got to Piccolos, a running group had taken over the sidewalk tables. I had to sit inside, which is more authentic Mimico than Europe. The lights are so bright you can see everyone's flaws. The baristas, bakers, and customers looked so ugly, so weathered. The radio was too loud. Everyone had to yell their orders over the soccer match. I didn't mind so much though. Working in a call centre, you learn to tune out anything. I bought a coffee and a Nutella donut and took my seat.

I was working on a spec for *Riders of Exley*. My mother's favourite show. My dream was to have my name in the credits one day and surprise her. A spec is basically when you write an episode of a TV show in hopes of getting hired on as a writer. It wasn't likely anyone would hire me. My ideas were no good. I'd been working on different *Riders of Exley* scripts for two years. I just couldn't get it right. Something was always off. Actually, everything was off. I'd work myself up into these frenzies. When I finished a new draft, I'd think it was decent. Possibly brilliant. And then I'd type up a cover letter, stuff it in a manila envelope, and skip off to the post office. Send my work into the void. I'd never heard back. Sometimes I pictured a mole-like executive with hairy fists and a huge cigar reading my work to his mistress in a hotel room, laughing at me. I was making progress though. Getting better. I liked writing my scripts. Eventually, I'd have one that was perfect. Even if it took twenty, thirty years. Of course, Mother likely wouldn't be around then and wouldn't see my name in the credits like I fantasized.

Also, the show would surely be off the air. But at least I'd have accomplished something.

I opened my notebook. *Riders of Exley* was a CBC drama about an English-style horse-riding school in the fictional Saskatchewan town of Cloud River. Kind of a coming-of-age thing. The series protagonist, Mary Valentine, arrives at Exley Riding School in the pilot when she's thirteen. She has her first period on one of the school's saddles, if that gives you an idea. But in the latest season, season three, the creators started incorporating these supernatural elements into the show. Like Mary's horse that died in the season one finale comes back as a ghost, helps her with her problems. Or this new student, Bertram, turns out to have ESP. I'd only recently added a fantastical element to my own script. Originally, my spec was about Mary confronting the school's bully, Stacy Maude Green. Mary finds out about Stacy's own troubled history and the two girls learn to respect each other. People really loved the ghost and ESP stuff, though, so now I had one of the students witness a glowing ball of light fly through the livery at night. The next morning all the horses have these marks on their backs. And they're all evil now. Biting the kids, running too fast, bucking. I just needed a clean way to tie it into my bullying story.

I started writing TV episodes while I was living on The Farm. Father Woodbine's cult was deeply depressing, once the initial veneer of positivity and acceptance I'd been welcomed with wore off. Woodbine never assaulted any of us, physically. As far as I know anyway. None of his older associates ever touched me inappropriately. Psychologically, however, we were all subjected to horrendous stuff. After a few months, I needed an escape from the dark world view that dominated the place. I wanted to watch TV, but we weren't allowed, so I started sneaking off to the bathroom to write my own versions of the shows I missed watching, like *Frasier* and *Ally McBeal*, on scrap paper.

Woodbine's ideas all circled around death. He said that society tried to shut out death, ignore it, act like it wasn't real. But he said death is an important part of life, something we need to accept and even embrace. We Citizens of Light, Woodbine declared, would stare into the face of death and recognize the light of God. The God-Spirit Ka-Ni was made up of two angels at war with each other: Ka, the Sun Spirit, and Ni, the Moon Spirit. One night Woodbine dreamt that the angels Ka and Ni were engaged in battle when their spirits collided and fell into a wellspring in Cairo. The combined God-Spirit, Ka-Ni, spoke to Woodbine in the dreamworld: "Life on Earth is an artificial approximation of God's true light. The natural light of God is death." The God-Spirit told him to start a church. Every night, Ka-Ni would enter Woodbine's sleeping brain and fill it with new teachings. As Woodbine's followers grew, these teachings became increasingly morbid. We had to dig trenches in the ground and then sleep in them on full moon nights. We watched videos of people getting shot, euthanized by doctors, and decapitated by terrorists. One time he had us steal a body from a nearby cemetery, which we kept in the shed for months until the cops showed up. Woodbine would lock me in the shed with the corpse, alone, for hours at a time.

When I returned home from The Farm, the death-obsessed teachings of the cult stayed with me. I couldn't stop thinking about dead bodies and the finality of my existence. I was ultra-aware of my lungs filling with and releasing air, my heart pumping blood, and how easily it could all stop. A psychologist helped me tamp down the endless cycle of death thoughts, but that wasn't enough. Writing my own TV episodes had become a coping mechanism. I relied on it to shut out the darkness of the world. No matter what was happening in my life, no matter how awful or sad, I could control the television characters in my notebook.

I nibbled on my Nutella donut and combed my mind for *Riders of Exley* ideas. More joggers entered the café. The room smelled like jogger sweat and fried sugar. A woman with beautiful bangs sat at the table across from me and had a phone conversation with Costco customer service. I guess she couldn't find her Gatorades when she got home from the store. The door to the shop was propped open and at one point a bird flew into the café. The woman with the bangs took a video of it with her phone. The bird was picking at crumbs by the pastry case.

"Look over here," the woman said. "Look at me."

I wasn't getting anywhere with my spec. I'd written down, "The horses go back to normal when Mary and Stacy hug." That's it. I couldn't concentrate. All I could think about was Niagara Falls. The man in the *Metro*.

I missed having Leonard's input on my TV scripts. Every now and then, if he was home after dinner, we'd go into the bedroom and I'd read him whatever I was working on at the time. Leonard would lie in the bed with his head propped up on three pillows. I'd sit at my desk and read from the laptop. He always said encouraging things. Every new script or draft I read to him was the best one yet, my finest work, brilliant, absolutely brilliant. He'd laugh at the jokes and sometimes he'd jump out of the bed and grip me in a congratulatory hug after I'd finished reading.

To be honest, though, I sometimes got the feeling that he wasn't really listening. That he was checked out and simply saying bland, nice things when it seemed appropriate to chime in. He had this vacant stare. Especially over the course of the last year. It was like he was becoming more withdrawn. Tired all the time. Irritable. But Leonard was often run down from the long hours he worked at the plastics plant. It made sense that he seemed a little removed, and anyway, my insecurities about my writing likely had me reading into things way too much. It was nice of Leonard to listen to my naïve little scripts, to encourage me.

I dropped my pen on the table and rubbed my eyes. It was Thursday. If I asked Ken for a weekend off, I'd be leaving in two weeks. *If* he said yes. But I couldn't wait two weeks. Not with that man hanging around casinos, posing for photographers in his idiotic vest. I had to go ASAP. I'd leave tomorrow. Ken had offered to give me the month off when Leonard died, and I hadn't taken it. I'd say I needed the weekend to grieve. That my grief was delayed. Maybe I could say I was attending a weekend retreat for young widows. Obviously, I couldn't tell him what I was really doing. Stalking some man from the newspaper. I'd sound crazy. Which maybe I was, I realized. But I still had to go.

I certainly couldn't involve the police. They didn't give a damn about Leonard. They thought he had killed himself. Which is insane. Leonard loved his life. I knew him. They didn't know him. Plus, the cops would muck everything up. If the man from the paper really did have something to do with Leonard's death, a detective coming around would only get his guard up. Finesse was required. Not that I had finesse, but I would try.

4

When I got home from work, I found Mother lying at the bottom of the basement stairs.

"Mother!"

"I'm alright," she said. "Having a little lie-down."

"At the bottom of the stairs?"

"I got tired. I was bringing the laundry down." Clothes and towels were strewn across the staircase, the laundry basket at Mother's feet.

"Did you fall?"

"No, I told you. I'm having a rest."

"Just say you fell. I *know* you fell down. There are clothes everywhere. Are you okay?"

"I'm fine, I'm fine. I dropped the laundry, yes. And then I thought I'd have a wee rest before I picked it all up."

"Oh God, Mother." I picked up the clothes on the stairs and brought them down. Then it dawned on me, the complications involved in a Niagara Falls trip. Mother had never been left alone longer than eight hours. Not since Leonard moved in with us, two years earlier. What if she fell while I was gone? There were a million things that could go wrong if I left her unsupervised.

"What am I going to do with you?" I started throwing the

clothes back in the basket. "Like, what would you do if I left you alone one weekend? For example?"

"Where are you going?" she asked. A look of terror on her face.

"Nowhere. I'm just wondering how you'd get along without me if I *did* go somewhere."

"Please, don't let me hold you back. You should take a vacation. I'm perfectly capable. Of course, it would break my heart to see you go. But that's silly. You deserve a nice trip. I hope you go away. I'll pay for it."

"Okay, but what if you fell down the stairs?"

"I didn't fall. I told you, I'm resting. Everything's perfect."

"Perfect, yes. Everything's perfect."

Mother had a hard time admitting when she needed help. She'd die before asking someone for something. She'd been a self-sufficient woman for most of her life. She raised me by herself. My father walked out on us when I was still a baby. I have no memory of him. He died of alcohol poisoning when I was three. Mother says she took me to his funeral, but I have no memory of that either. My birth certificate says Colleen Erickson, which was my father's surname. I took Mother's after he left us and grew up Colleen Paper. Now I'm Colleen Weagle, because of Leonard. So many names for one dull person. I'll take Weagle to my grave, though. Even if I marry someone else, which is unlikely, Weagle stays. Colleen Weagle feels like the name of my soul now.

I helped Mother up off the ground and walked her up the stairs, sat her on the couch. Turned on the Food Network. I couldn't leave her alone for too long, but I had to go to Niagara Falls. I couldn't bring her with me. She had knee issues, back issues. And I didn't want her to know what I was up to. She had enough worries. I couldn't ask the neighbours to look after her. We didn't know the neighbours. Mother and I kept to ourselves for the most part. They all had their own stuff going on and we had ours. Sometimes I chatted with Mr. Godfrey from across the street about the weather and his garden and the hot air balloons he saw over the weekend. But Mr. Godfrey was older than Mother and in worse shape. Bad eyesight, bad hearing, bad knees, and an ear-splitting cough. You could hear it from across the street on summer nights when our windows were open wide.

Maybe Patti could check in on her. Of course, that would cost me. She'd bleed me for whatever she could get. It was worth it though. I was heading to Niagara Falls the next day and that was that. At work that night I'd talk to Ken about getting emergency time off and I'd talk to Patti about Mother. I'd find the Metro Man. Find the truth. Then I'd come home, get back to work, and chip away at my scripts. In time things would settle. Everything wouldn't be *perfect*, like Mother said, but maybe everything would be pretty good. I had to try.

I took an earlier bus to work and approached Ken before the evening shift began. I decided to tell him I was going to Niagara to dump Leonard's ashes down the falls. I said it was his favourite place, that he went there when he was a kid and bonded with his dad, and that we had our first date there. A lie, of course. But the lie was tangled up with the truth of my real plan—that I was going to Niagara Falls on Leonard-related business—and so it would sound more believable coming out of my mouth.

"I just need tomorrow evening off and then Sunday," I said. Ken stared at his fingernails while I talked, his face expressionless. "Again, I'm so sorry for this late notice, but my mother sprang the bus ticket on me. The hotel is already booked."

"The thing is," Ken said, looking up from his nails, "we need you to give us two weeks. That's our policy."

"I know, but my mother sprang—"

"If we made an exception with you now, then we'd have to make an exception for the next person. Then the next person. Pretty soon, nobody would be making calls. It would just be me sitting here supervising a bunch of empty chairs. Right?"

"I guess so. Sure."

"Exactly. We're starting a new campaign for Bank of America tomorrow and we need you here, Colleen. You'll have fun with that one. I know it. Now if you'd like to go on a little trip some other weekend, fill out a Request for Time Off form, okay? And make sure to hand it in at least two weeks beforehand, unless you have a doctor's note. Alright? We're good?"

"Yes, sir."

"Great. Don't forget to punch in. Let's see if we can hit some big numbers tonight. I bet you'll crush this one!"

I was in a foul mood the rest of my shift. Not that I blamed Ken. He had a point. You can't have everyone skirting policy every time something personal pops up or the whole system would fall to pieces. Still, my brain felt blackened. Everything I looked at seemed charged with negative energy. My computer was full of hate. My headset was full of hate too. Every person and object in the vicinity hated all the other people and objects in the vicinity.

I made my calls, but I couldn't focus. I pulled my notebook out and tried to drum up new *Riders of Exley* ideas. Nothing came. I drew these horrible birds in the margins. They looked menacing. No one was really picking up the phone that night. It happens. I finished the *Metro* crossword in half an hour. Most of the night, I sat there staring at my screen, arms folded.

I finished at eleven, clocked out. Patti cornered me in the elevator.

"I suppose you want another ride," she said.

"I'm fine."

"Excuse me? You'd rather stand around a bus stop in the shadows? With a bunch of maniacs and rapists?"

"I don't know."

"What's wrong with you?"

"I'm sorry." We reached the ground floor, walked out toward the street. "I wanted to go to Niagara Falls this weekend to spread Leonard's ashes. They wouldn't give me the time off."

"What?" Patti grabbed my shoulders, looked into my eyes. Her breath smelled like the inside of her car. A mixture of gingerbread and wet towels. "You wanna go to Niagara Falls? Who'd you talk to? April?"

"Ken."

"That son of a bitch. What, they can't get by without you for one weekend? I'll throttle that little prick."

"No, it's okay. Honestly—"

"The hell it's okay. What, you're working Friday and Sunday?"

"Yeah."

"That's bullshit. Two frigging days. You're spreading Leonard's ashes for Christ's sake. Hold on, I'll go talk to him."

"No, Patti, please—"

"It's done."

She stepped back onto the elevator.

I waited.

When Patti returned, she slapped me on the back. "Looks like you owe me one," she said. "We're going to Niagara!"

"Really?"

"Of course. I got your back. Now let's get out of here. I'll drive you home. Tell you what, you don't need to pay me because I didn't give you change for yesterday. Already paid for."

"Thank you for talking to Ken. Thank you so much, Patti. Honestly."

"Of course."

"This really means a lot. But did you say *we're* going to Niagara?"

"Oh yes, I'm coming."

"You are?"

"Why not? Of course, I'm coming. I asked for the weekend off too. I haven't been to the casino in ages. It'll be fun. Anyway, how were you planning on getting there? The bus?"

"Well, yes. But I kind of thought—"

"It's a vacation, Colleen. You can't take the bus. Jesus. I'll drive us there. It'll be a girl's weekend. God, this'll be good. Do you have a hotel yet?"

"No, not yet."

"Well, pick something nice. Whatever you can afford. You cover that and the gas, we can call it even."

"You're coming with me?"

"God, Colleen. Do you even realize how rude you sound? Yes, I'm fucking coming. We'll have a girl's weekend. You can't spread Leonard's ashes alone. Let's go already. I wanna get home so I can tell Dougie."

5

I spent the rest of the night packing. I filled my bag with the usual vacation supplies—clothes, makeup, tampons, phone charger, a Mars bar, a Snickers bar, two Nature Valley granola bars, and my screenplay notebook. I considered bringing a few special items to help with my mission. Black attire, in case I had to follow the Metro Man at night. See where he lived before I confronted him. A flashlight, for snooping through his home. Of course, it was likely I'd just find him at work, take him aside, and craftily get him to shed light on Leonard's death through conversation alone. I had to be prepared for anything, though. And maybe it really would be better to gather intelligence first. See what I was dealing with before meeting this weasel face to face.

You don't know anything about my husband's death, do you? I'd ask. *Well then what were* these *doing in your car?* I'd hold up a plastic baggie with leaves from the bog in it. They wouldn't even have to be from the bog. He just had to think I had some kind of real evidence. I could picture the man's expression. Like a fat Mimico raccoon when you catch it digging through your bin on trash night.

In the end, I threw a dark green sweatshirt in my bag. Just in case. I put the flashlight back in the wall charger, Leonard's ski mask in his winter basket. No need to go overboard.

I wrote up a weekend itinerary for Mother. Patti had horned in on my trip and I couldn't think of anyone else who would watch her on short notice, so I decided *I* would watch her. Via the itinerary. I'd keep her busy with simple activities like reading the first chapter of *Under the Dome* or watering the fern in my bedroom. She'd have to check in with me—phone calls were on the schedule. Naps, TV programs, all of it. I organized everything so that Mother would have a fun, relaxing, and productive weekend. I copied it out twice: one for the fridge, and one that Mother could carry from room to room. I kept the original. In case of an emergency, I'd asked Mr. Godfrey from across the street for his phone number. Most likely he wouldn't hear his phone going off, but having the number provided some small comfort.

"You're really going?" Mother asked. Friday morning. I had my backpack ready on the porch. Patti was already twenty minutes late.

"You'll be fine. Trust me. Follow the itinerary. I'll call you in a few hours."

"You don't have to worry about me, dear. I'm perfectly fine. I just hope you're not leaving because of me. I know I've been a handful."

"I'm just spending some time with Patti. It's a girl's weekend." I actually was excited to hang out with Patti away from work. She can be a bit of a pain, but there's something admirable about the way she moves through the world. If something's bothering her, she calls it out. If she wants something, she grabs for it. Perhaps by sharing a hotel room with Patti I'd absorb some of her attitude, her swagger. It would help me with my mission.

"You know, you don't have to call me," Mother said.

"What are you talking about?"

"I think you shouldn't bother calling. You're on vacation. I'll bring you down. Go have fun, we'll talk when you're back. In fact, I won't answer the phone."

"If you don't answer the phone, I'm driving back immediately."

"Oh, Colleen. I would *die* if you came back early. Because of me."

"Then answer the phone."

Patti pulled up an hour late. She said she had car troubles but refused to elaborate. The car seemed fine. I didn't press the issue—what did I care? I was on my way to Niagara Falls. Soon I'd find out what had happened to poor Leonard. I felt like I was in charge. Like the universe had been whipping me for the past three months and now I'd caught the whip in my hand. Yanked it away from the universe. Raising my eyebrows and grinning at the universe with this insane confidence.

"Let's listen to something," Patti said.

"Sure! Whatever you choose is fine."

"Of course it's fine. This is my car."

"I only meant—"

"There's a CD set in the glove compartment."

I reached in and grabbed the set—an audiobook from the library.

"Columbine?"

"That's it. Disc one."

"Is this about Columbine, like the school shooting?"

"Of course. Jesus."

"Isn't this a little dark for a road trip?"

"Oh grow up. It's an interesting story and I've been looking forward to listening to it. You'll love it. You're not going to be like this the whole weekend, are you?"

"I'm sorry."

I found disc one, popped it in the player. Patti was in a mood. She had this discolouration on her cheek, like a bruise she'd tried to cover with makeup. A bruise like that would put me in a mood too. Poor Patti. I had a special skill, anyway: patience. Mother once told me that God sometimes appears on Earth, disguised as other people. To test you. If you're patient with people and you don't get all flustered when they're in moods, like Patti, you can show God or whatever energy form you worship how strong you really are.

We drove through Oakville and Burlington. Leonard was born in Oakville. The plastics plant he worked at was in Burlington. One time I took the train and met him after his shift. We had dinner at a spaghetti place near the plant. Leonard was convinced that O.J. Simpson was sitting at one of the other tables—it wasn't him. We argued about that while we ate, whispering our points, but it was still a great dinner. Leonard and I always got along, even when we weren't getting along. If that makes sense. We respected each other. I looked out the window for the spaghetti place but didn't recognize anything.

We stopped at a Wendy's in Hamilton so I could pee. Patti told me to be quick, but the toilet seat was disgusting so I had to layer it with toilet paper, and the automatic flusher kept sucking it all down into the bowl.

Back in the parking lot, I saw that Patti was on the phone. It looked like she was crying. Her face was redder than usual. Maybe that was just the light coming through the car window though. I walked around the building a few times until she honked, then I jumped back in the car.

"Everything okay?"

"Mind your business." Patti turned the Columbine book up full. The dashboard rattled. The narrator talked about one of the shooters making pipe bombs in his parents' basement. Patti said more things, but I couldn't hear her over the book. She used curse words. We got back on the highway.

As we closed in on our destination, I began to sweat. It was all too real. It's easy to imagine going to some strange city, confronting strange men. But when you're actually doing it, everything changes. I didn't care about what had happened to my husband anymore. I honestly didn't. To hell with it all, I thought. I'm not talking to some goon in a casino. Besides, the man from the funeral was probably Leonard's shy old acquaintance. He didn't know anything. The whole trip was a psychotic break. But the car was moving forward with me in it, there wasn't anything I could do. Maybe I could just follow Patti around for the weekend, get through it. Snap a few pictures. Shop for souvenirs. Back to work on Monday. Forget everything.

We drove through Grimsby. I told Patti that Grimsby sounds like a dwarf name, or a gnome. I thought it was a funny joke we could riff on together, but she didn't hear me. We were on disc two of the Columbine book. I tried not to listen because it was upsetting, but details kept getting through. Heartbreaking backstories of the victims. I imagined that the book's author had made everything up, that they were a bad reporter.

I read all the signs. One said, BIRD KINGDOM KEEP LEFT. Then we drove over this long, gorgeous bridge. It took five minutes to get across, or it felt like five. I couldn't believe it. We passed a wind farm. I saw a senior citizen lifting weights on his lawn. If you step outside of your head and really look around, the world is filled with beautiful things.

6

I imagined Niagara Falls as this town where you could see the actual waterfalls no matter where you stood. Like the falls tower over everything. The way a child might picture Niagara Falls. But it's just a normal city. You have to go to the falls to see the falls. We drove to our hotel and the town looked like Burlington or Oakville or even Mimico.

"This is where we're staying?" Patti said.

We parked in front of the Captain's Inn. It looked like a dentist's office. Just off the highway, surrounded by other, similar-looking hotels. Off-white plaster, two floors. A small pool in the parking lot. A giant billboard for Montana's BBQ & Bar cast a shadow over the water.

"Captain's Inn. Yes, this is it."

"This is disappointing."

We went inside with our bags, and I gave the kid at the counter my credit card. The kid was eating a sandwich. When he handed back my card, there was mayonnaise on it.

We walked down a dim hallway that smelled like cigarettes, then up a staircase. I wondered if Leonard had ever stayed in a hotel like this when he came to Niagara Falls. If he came to Niagara Falls. Or maybe he had even stayed at the Captain's Inn—maybe he had the same room. Our room was next to the staircase. 201. I opened the door and Patti charged in. She threw her luggage on one twin bed and then flopped herself down on the other.

The room was thin and long. The carpet an unpleasant shade of brown. A wooden desk in one corner, a TV on another desk farther down the wall. An old metal baby crib by the window—it looked like a raccoon trap. The lamps beside the beds had clear plastic coverings over the shades.

"What a piece of shit," Patti said. "I can't breathe."

The air was stale and hot. I went over to the window—sealed shut. I turned the AC on, and this horrible stench filled the room instantly. Like an old, sickly dog breathing into your mouth.

The smell eventually dissipated. It wasn't so bad, actually. Patti took a nap and I called Mother from the bathroom. I turned on the shower so Patti wouldn't hear me. I reached Mother's voicemail three times before she finally picked up.

"Colleen?"

"Why didn't you pick up? I've been calling and calling."

"It wasn't on the schedule. I was supposed to be drinking lemonade on the porch. It's noon now, which is when we're supposed to talk. So, I picked up."

"Well, I'm glad you're sticking to the schedule. But geez. Did you drink lemonade on the porch?"

"I'm sorry, honey. I didn't feel like lemonade. Also, I didn't go to the store earlier, so we don't have any."

"Right."

"By the way, a man stopped by the house a little while ago and asked for you."

"Who?"

"He didn't say. He asked if you were home. I said you were away for the weekend, and he asked where, so I said Niagara Falls. And then he just walked off. Is that okay? Should I not have told him?"

"What did he look like?"

"He was big. Like a football player. Maybe an old friend from school?"

"I don't know. I don't really know anyone like that. Did he say anything else?"

"No, just what I told you. He asked where you were and then took off."

"Strange. Let me know if he comes back."

Mother said she'd keep me updated. We said goodbye. I turned off the shower but sat back down on the toilet cover. Who was this large man and why was he looking for me? Why *now*? I never had visitors. I didn't know any football players. Maybe Mother had dreamt the whole thing.

When Patti woke up an hour later, we walked down to the falls. The hotel receptionist said it would take us twenty minutes, but it was more like fifty. Most of it spent along the highway, the sun beating down on us. We were both soaked with sweat.

I got this feeling the Metro Man would suddenly appear. He could easily walk out of one of the hotels or step out from a cab. I was in his town. I could potentially be confronted at any second with this person who knew the truth about Leonard. But it wasn't a comforting thought. I was spooked. I didn't want to see this man. Best-case scenario, my mission would fail. I'd spend my weekend with Patti, undisturbed, and then go back to Mimico just as clueless as when I'd left. So then why was I here? I thought. What was the point?

When we got to the falls though—my God. I'd never seen anything like it. I'd looked at pictures, but you can't tell from pictures how big the falls really are. How majestic. I cried. Then Patti pointed out that I was looking at the American side and turned me in the direction of the Canadian falls, which were even more majestic. This was what I'd seen in all those photographs. Horseshoe Falls. I was crying and sweating, and I almost collapsed right there on the sidewalk.

There were other tourists lined up along the railing overlooking the falls, seagulls swarming overhead. People taking pictures. So many people. I couldn't believe it. Once, when I was in sixth grade, I was walking home from school and a police officer passed by on a horse. As he passed, the horse turned and looked at me. We stared into each other's eyes for what felt like a full minute. It was overwhelming in the same way the falls were overwhelming. I couldn't believe that what stood in front of me was actually there. I felt inspired. I would succeed in my mission.

"This is so real," I said to Patti.

"Uh huh," she said. "Let's go to the casino."

"I could look at this for hours and hours."

"*Casino*, Colleen. Let's move it along."

I could always go back later. We were there for a whole weekend. We walked back up the winding sidewalk toward the main street, where all the fancy hotels stood. When we passed this gorgeous fountain filled with nickels and dimes, I dipped my hands in and poured the fountain water down the back of my shirt.

"Come on," Patti said, "let's go in."

"Really?" I assumed she was talking about the fountain. Like we should climb in and swim around. "I don't know."

"Come on. The entrance is over there." Patti pointed to a series of glass doors on the other side of the fountain, up the drive.

Fallsview Casino.

I held my breath as we walked through the big glass doors to the casino. The man from Leonard's funeral could potentially be standing on the other side. Of course, the doors were transparent, so I knew he wasn't standing *right* there. Somewhere close by, though. But the doors didn't lead right into the casino. We were in a kind of shopping mall atrium. High-end clothing shops, purses, diamonds. Somewhere to spend your winnings should you be impatient. A last-ditch effort by the casino to keep customers' money on the property. The real entrance to the casino was next to a watch store and the lineup to get inside was long—and getting longer.

Patti and I joined the queue. The line snaked around a curved wall, and when we reached the halfway point, I could see attendants checking IDs up ahead. We shuffled forward, slowly. My phone buzzed.

"I'll meet you inside," I told Patti, then stepped back out into the atrium.

"Colleen, this is Ken from the office. You're an hour late. What's going on?"

"Excuse me?"

"You're late. I'm looking at your chair right now. You're not in it. Last I checked, your chair won't complete surveys by itself. Are you on your way?"

"But I have the weekend off."

"You most certainly do not. I remember our conversation quite clearly. This is unacceptable behaviour. I'm looking at your empty chair right now. Chairs don't complete surveys."

"Patti told me she talked to you."

"Is Patti with you? I was going to call her next. This is ridiculous. We're down two diallers and Bank of America is starting tonight. How soon can you get here?"

I hung up.

I rejoined the line for the casino. Patti was long gone. I couldn't believe it. She'd told me I had the weekend off.

I waited. A woman in a brown blazer glanced at my driver's license and waved me through.

My first time inside a real casino. I whispered "wow" slowly, like some moron. Like a rube. It was all so overwhelming. There were seemingly thousands of slot machines, stretching back farther than I could see. It was like a glitzy forest in a futuristic dream. The noise was instantly mesmerizing. All the machines chiming away. It sounded like millions of tiny harps talking to each other in heaven.

I could have stood there in wonderment for hours, but I had to find Patti. I walked down an aisle of TV show–themed slot machines—*Big Bang Theory, Sex and the City*—and kept watch for Patti and the man from the *Metro*.

I had pictured Fallsview as this classy joint, like in the movies. *Ocean's Eleven* with Brad Pitt and Clooney. Women in ball gowns and glittering jewels, the men in tuxes. Soft jazz. Witty remarks around green tables. Champagne. But people were wearing shorts and fanny packs. NASCAR visors. Clunky plastic running shoes. They sat back in their chairs, staring dead-eyed at the machines. They looked like bored babies. The machines had these cranks you could pull to spin the pictures, like how you see them on TV, but everyone tapped a button instead. I wasn't being judgmental—I certainly wasn't wearing a ball gown. I had on shorts and a pink ballcap. It was interesting though. A little surprising. I was learning so much about the world, and I hadn't been away from Toronto a full day yet.

I texted Patti, then began my search for the Metro Man. I wasn't sure what to do when I saw him. Be direct? Speak in riddles? Maybe I'd know what to do once we were face to face. A solid plan would reveal itself to me in the moment.

There was a lot of ground to cover. The casino was enormous. Like one of those parking garages that go on and on. He could be working a blackjack table, or he could be a bartender. Perhaps a washroom attendant, or door security, or maybe he made change for people. All these different jobs. All these vests walking around. There were smaller, exclusive rooms off the main room too. I could potentially take all afternoon or even the evening to find him.

And that was assuming he still worked at the casino, and that he was working that afternoon. I floated along the carpet, searching the crowds.

First, I stuck close to the wall and walked the perimeter of the giant room. Then I weaved through the aisles of slot machines. I kept passing the same employees in vests, and I stared at them with suspicion. They all stared right back. I must have looked like I was up to something, which in a way I was. None of them had attended Leonard's funeral. No sign of Patti either.

I sat down at a slot machine. *Masters of Magic*. I needed a moment. It had been a long day and it was hardly halfway through. I thought about playing *Masters of Magic*, but I couldn't figure out where to put my money. There didn't seem to be a coin slot.

I zoned out for a bit. I guess I didn't realize how exhausted I was from all the excitement of the day. I daydreamed I was chasing a rabbit through a field of tall grass, like what a dog would dream. A sharp pain brought me back to reality and Patti was standing above me, drink in hand. She'd pressed her cold glass up against my arm.

"You okay?" she asked.

"I couldn't find you," I said. "Ken called me. Ken from work."

"Oh yeah?"

"He said I was late. He said I didn't have the weekend off. He was really mad."

"That's funny. What an asshole."

"Okay, but I thought you talked to him."

"We're here now. Nothing you nor I can do about it."

"But you said—"

"Forget about it. Ken has to cover his ass and call, right? He called. It's over. We'll go back to work on Monday and he won't even remember."

"But you said that he said that we had the weekend off."

"So you misheard me. Or whatever. Anyway, who was that old man?"

"What old man?"

"The one you were talking to before I came over."

"What do you mean? I wasn't talking to anyone."

"He was standing right here, where I am. Real old. Had a tuxedo on. I mean, it sure looked like he was talking to you. Were you asleep?"

"No. I guess I wasn't paying attention. Maybe he was waiting for the machine."

"Maybe. But it didn't look like that. He was staring at you, all intense. I thought you were having an argument."

"Do you see him anywhere?"

I stood up and Patti and I looked around the room for an old man in a tuxedo. I didn't see him.

"Guess he's gone," Patti said. "Oh well. I'm starving. Let's go eat."

"What about the old man?

"What about him? He's gone now. Probably some creep. I bet this place is crawling with old pervs. Anyway, I'm starving. Let's move."

7

We went to Jimmy Buffett's Margaritaville and ate peppercorn burgers. We talked about exploring the town after dinner, but by the time the bill arrived we were both exhausted. Patti had lost sixty bucks on slots and I felt bad, so I paid. I had a vague idea of my chequing account's balance but was afraid to look. Best to forge ahead and deal with difficulties as they arose. We taxied back to the Captain's Inn. Another twenty bucks.

Patti fell asleep immediately. I turned out the lights and stared at my phone. Three missed calls from work. A problem for another day. In half an hour, Mother would call. According to the schedule at least. The hotel's Wi-Fi kept cutting out—I couldn't even check my email. Although I had yet to receive any kind of response to the spec scripts I sent out, it could potentially happen at any moment and I checked often. Even a flat-out rejection would be encouraging. My inbox was full of newsletters from First Choice, my haircutting place.

My body was tired, but my mind was rattling along, full speed. I went into the bathroom with my spec notebook. I couldn't focus. I kept thinking about Leonard. I wrote LEONARD on the page in block letters. I thought about how fun it would have been to visit Niagara Falls with him. Not that there was anything wrong with

Patti—we were getting along fine. But Leonard and I never took a vacation together. No trips. My paycheque barely covered our bills, and Leonard had this outrageous student debt. We mostly watched TV together.

I met Leonard online through a dating site I heard about on the evening news. They interviewed this man who had created a profile on the site, started talking to this woman, and then the woman somehow got all his information and stole his identity. There was a picture of the man, and he was gorgeous. Like Tom Bergeron. I made my own profile, hoping to meet someone like the beautiful scam victim. I met Leonard.

Leonard didn't look anything like Tom Bergeron, but he was handsome in his own way. Rail-thin, which suited him. Strong jaw. He'd lost most of his hair but he had a beautifully shaped head so it didn't matter. Funny little teeth. He liked to wear these papery work shirts with short sleeves, like a Cuban businessman on a boat. That's what he said he was going for anyway. The bottom of the shirt would flap around his ribs in the wind. I grew to be quite attracted to him.

I was nervous about meeting Leonard for the first time. I hadn't dated anyone in years. Eight years, to be exact. I shied away from all that, preferring to keep my life simple, but the idea of going on a date with Leonard excited me. He seemed sweet from our little chats on the dating site. We mostly talked about our jobs—I had just started at the call centre at the time and Leonard had been working at the plastics plant a few years already.

For our first date, Leonard took me to the library near his apartment. They were showing *Marley & Me*, projected onto the wall of a study room. We sat in folding chairs. Ten minutes in, some construction project started up in an adjacent room—hammering, an electric drill. The librarian in charge of the event paused the film and went off to get them to stop. Leonard and I sat silently for twenty minutes, until the librarian came back and resumed the movie. I looked over now and then and Leonard seemed terrified, his hands shaking in his lap. Afterward, Leonard took me over to the CD racks and pointed out all his favourite bands. Sweat dripped from his forehead. I pretended to know nothing about the Beach Boys, even though I knew some. He got me to borrow a compilation of their hits. Then he walked me back to my bus stop. I told him about a dream I'd had the night before, where I couldn't find a bathroom. Leonard stared into my eyes when I spoke, nodding along. I struggled to think of other things to say. I said I liked the movie, but it was a little sad. He agreed. A long minute passed in silence. Leonard asked me if I'd always lived in Toronto, and I told him that I had. He nodded. I looked down at my feet. And then I brought up The Farm. How I'd technically lived outside of the city for eight months as a teenager. I didn't really want to get into all that, but it was true and our struggle to keep a conversation going was making me uncomfortable. Most people found the cult stuff interesting. It would give us enough material to work with until my bus arrived.

"No," Leonard said. His eyes seemed to be poking out farther. Like two white dogs pulling on their leashes. "I remember that story from the news."

"You do?"

"Oh yes, I remember looking at the pictures in the paper and on TV and imagining what it was like to live there. The Citizens of Light. The Citizens of Light Rejuvenation Farm. That must have been so hard. I'm so sorry."

"That was a long time ago."

"Still. I'm sorry, Colleen. That awful, awful man."

My bus pulled up. Other people got on, but we ignored it, watched it drive off.

It really meant something to me, the way Leonard responded to my story. He immediately focused on my feelings, my pain.

Whenever I brought The Farm up—and I usually avoided the topic entirely—most people wanted to hear the grisly details. They wanted to know about the body snatching or the other disturbing rituals Father Woodbine made us take part in, as if these things were exciting. Like they were getting off on hearing about my trauma. Leonard actually cared.

I cried a little and then Leonard put his arm around me. We stood there quietly. "Let's change the subject," Leonard said. He shot off some more interesting Beach Boys facts. Brian Wilson was deaf in one ear. Dennis Wilson hung out with the Manson Family. We sat down on a strip of grass by the bus stop and talked about the Beach Boys, TV, and our lives in general. I told him about my spec scripts and he seemed genuinely interested. He told me a little about his upbringing: how he was abandoned by his father, then his mother, then kicked around to different relatives, foster parents, and, eventually, juvenile detention centres. I'd later learn that his twenties were spent feeding various addictions. He'd devoted the last decade to living clean and trying to build a quiet, stable life for himself.

Recounting his childhood, Leonard choked up. I cried too, again. It was pretty emotional for a first date. We let two more buses come and go before I stood up to get on a third. I let Leonard kiss me, even with the driver watching. That's how it all started for me and Leonard.

A half hour passed. Mother was supposed to call but my phone was silent. I was sitting on the toilet, the ceiling fan groaning above me. I waited fifteen more minutes and then called home.

No answer.

I waited a few minutes, called again. Same thing—she didn't pick up. I called continuously for ten minutes. I paced around the tiny bathroom.

I knew this was going to happen, I thought. She'd ruined everything. Leonard's death would remain a mystery. I had to go back to Mimico. Mother would be fine, of course. Probably. Avoiding my calls for some complicated, guilt-driven reason. But there was a chance she wasn't okay. Maybe she fell. She could be lying there, alone. Dehydrated. Concussed. I thought of poor Leonard in Morrison Bog.

I tried Mr. Godfrey, our elderly neighbour, and got his machine. I left a frantic, rambling message for him to check on Mother and then call me with the update, but I wasn't holding my breath that he'd ever hear it.

There was nothing I could do—the trip was over.

I poked at Patti's feet with a Bird Kingdom pamphlet. She sat up and stared at me like I was insane.

"Do you have any idea what kind of dream you just interrupted?" Patti snarled.

"Sorry. But listen. I need to go back."

"I don't want to get graphic, but these two airport security guys—"

"Patti. Please. I'm going back to Toronto. My mother's not answering the phone."

"So what?" Patti sat up on her elbows, squinting at me angrily in the dim room.

"Patti—"

"I'm not driving you. You can walk yourself to the bus station. This is supposed to be a girls' weekend for Christ's sake. You're *abandoning* me."

"I'm sorry but I have to go. She might have fallen or had some accident. I'm really sorry."

"I can't believe this. You are ridiculous. You know what? No. I'm putting my foot down. Call someone or whatever, but you are not leaving me here alone. This is my trip too. No way."

"Hey!" I grabbed the bottom of the comforter at the foot of Patti's bed and tore it off her, slapped it onto the carpet. I'm not sure what came over me. It happened in an instant. My arms were shaking.

"I'm leaving," I said. "Deal with it."

Patti didn't respond. She looked genuinely frightened. She'd never seen me in such a state. Neither had I, for that matter. I grabbed my bag and my notebook and stomped out of the room.

8

I walked in the direction of the casino. I didn't know where the bus station was located but I figured I'd happen upon it, or I'd ask someone. I tried Mother again—no answer.

I half expected Patti to come running after me. She'd apologize first, then I'd apologize. A warm, sisterly hug. I kept looking back over my shoulder. The sun continued to blast down on the sidewalks and my shirt became soaked for the second time that day. I'd have to change it in the station bathroom before I boarded my bus home.

I remembered the time Mother ripped away my comforter and yelled at me, just like I had done with Patti. I guess I'd learned the trick from her. This was in high school, before I'd ended up on The Farm with Father Woodbine. Mother had found cigarettes and a little bottle of Irish whiskey in my backpack. I woke up in a panic—the sudden cold, Mother's screeching. "Do you want to end up like your father?" I started screaming and Mother locked herself in her bedroom. Sobbing loudly into her pillow. I'd forgotten all about that morning. It was hard to square that version of Mother with the one I lived with now, who would never even think about raising her voice.

I walked along the highway. Traffic roared by. I called Mother. No bus station in sight. I eventually made it to the casino. I stopped at the fountain out front, dipped my hands in, flicked water onto my neck and temples, then entered the shopping atrium. A woman sitting on a bench was fanning her crotch with one of her flip-flops. I sat down beside her and caught my breath. My calf muscles ached. The woman stood up from the bench and walked away half-barefoot, still holding one flip-flop in her hand. I smelled terrible, I realized. I rooted around in my backpack in search of my deodorant stick, but it wasn't there. It was in the bathroom at the hotel. I'd abandoned my deodorant too.

I felt bad about how I'd left things with Patti. The girls' weekend had been ruined. At the same time, though, I also felt kind of good. The look on her face. Her blanket on the floor. I felt like Ms. Klein, the headmistress on *Riders of Exley*, dressing down the students. Nobody crossed Ms. Klein. She wore her hair in a tight, intimidating bun. Maybe I'd start wearing my hair in a bun too.

I stood in line for the casino. The plan was to ask the attendant about the bus station when they checked my ID. When the attendant called me forward, however, I flashed my driver's license and wordlessly stepped out onto the casino floor. The mesmerizing slot machine music. The lights, the colours, the zigzag carpet.

I knew I needed to get out of there and hurry to the bus station, but I was also overheated and thirsty. The cool casino air felt so soothing. If I ordered a glass of water, I could ask about the buses. And it would be perfectly fine if I had a quick look around the room while I made my way toward the bar.

I scanned the area, but the man from the newspaper wasn't in sight. No old men in tuxedos either. I saw a woman in a brown pantsuit on her knees, looking at the carpet through a magnifying glass. Like she'd lost a tiny diamond. Another woman stopped me to ask for the time but walked off while I was digging through my bag for my phone. It was in my pocket.

I sidled up to the circular bar and waited for one of the bartenders to notice me. An elderly woman tapped at an electronic blackjack game embedded in the counter. A man in a *Bee Movie* ball cap stood a few feet away, staring at me. The little straw from his drink hung from his lip like a cigarette. I tried Mother again, but she wasn't answering. I considered texting Patti. But she should be the one to reach out first, I thought. My mother was in peril, possibly. I decided to be patient and give Patti a chance to apologize. She'd come around.

The bartender came over and I asked him for water and directions. He drew a little map to the station on a cocktail napkin. It was past the Captain's Inn. I'd have to taxi. The bartender was walking away when an idea came to me. I had the *Metro* clipping in my bag.

"Hold on," I said. "Excuse me, sir?"

And then I pulled out the clipping, slid it across the bar. The bartender picked it up and squinted.

"The man in the Fallsview vest," I said. "You see? Kind of in the back."

"Sure."

"Do you know this man? He works here."

He studied the photo. "Hmm, no. Don't think so."

"Oh. Thank you anyway."

"Well, wait. I'm on-call. Let me ask Ryan. He's here all the time. Hey, Ryan!"

The other bartender walked over. The first bartender showed him the picture, pointed out the man from Leonard's funeral.

"I'm trying to find that man. Do you know him?" I asked.

Ryan frowned at the picture, then looked up and frowned at me.

"Sorry, no. Who is this?"

"Brother-in-law." I'm not sure why I lied. It seemed safer, somehow.

"Brother-in-law," Ryan said. "I have a brother-in-law myself. Great guy. This is from last week, right? The arrest?"

"Yes."

"Strange. Yeah, I've never seen him. You'd think we would've crossed paths at some point."

"But maybe he's just in another department?"

"Sure, yeah. It's quite an operation we have here. You wouldn't believe how many employees. Pretty strange though. I thought I knew everyone. Someone around here ought to know him though. What's his name, Miss?"

"I don't know."

"You don't know your brother-in-law's name?"

"We're not that close."

"I'm sorry?"

I leaned over, snatched the clipping back from Ryan, and started walking away from the bar.

"Miss?" Ryan called. "Hey!"

I didn't turn around.

9

The bus home was a double-decker. So many new experiences that day. I decided to go up top and enjoy the luxurious view, but as soon as I sat down, I felt pre-nauseous—like I could tell nausea was on its way. My situation was serious: rushing home early from a trip to potentially find my mother keeled over at the bottom of the stairs, her phone blinking on the carpet, just out of reach. It would be better to keep my head down and focus on the sombre reality of the circumstance. On my way back down the tiny stair-case, a large group of teenagers came stomping up and I had to turn around and re-ascend. I found a seat in the back and the teens piled in around me, pinning me in place.

I leaned into the window and called Mother again. It would be just like her to pick up now that I'd boarded the bus and was trapped in my seat, but she didn't. Then I tried our neighbour again. Answering machine. The bus backed out of the lot, moved toward the highway.

I could phone Ken, I realized. Obviously not the ideal option considering I'd accidentally skipped out on work, hung up on him, and then ducked his numerous calls. But I felt so helpless. I had to do something.

"Innovative Business Standards, Ken speaking."

"Hi, Ken. It's Colleen Weagle."

"Well look who decides to finally call. This better be good. I honestly can't wait to hear your explanation. In fact, maybe I'll go make some popcorn. Do you mind holding?"

"I need you to do me a favour."

"A favour? Did you honestly just ask me for a favour?"

Ken broke into this fake, indignant chuckle. I interrupted him. "Listen!" I yelled. The fake laughter stopped abruptly. The teens went quiet, too. I didn't care. "I need you to check in on my mother. I'm out of town and she's not answering her phone. She's on a new medication. She might have fallen. I'm going to give you my address now."

"HR actually has it on file—"

"Just write it down."

Ken agreed to stop by the house. He promised to go once April, the other supervisor, returned from her dinner break.

For a brief moment, I forgot about my anxiety and revelled in my new powers. Ken had completely backed down. It's like I'd been this sad old laundry heap for so long that I was able to catch people like Ken and Patti off guard by suddenly turning serious and authoritative. They weren't sure how to react. It was a new feeling and I liked it. As if I were a foot taller.

We drove on. Half the teenagers fell asleep. The other half spoke to each other softly, respectful of their companions, I thought. The future was bright. We passed a field with a real, classic scarecrow—unless it was a man in a hat standing around. Strip malls. Back over that impressive bridge. A Petro-Canada sign read: HAPPY BDAY BABY JEWEL ½ PRICE CINN HEARTS.

I thought about what I'd learned in Fallsview. The full-time bartender didn't recognize the man in the photo. The casino employed a ton of people, but still. Something felt off. Maybe the Metro Man didn't actually work there. Maybe he wore their uniform as a disguise. If so, it likely had something to do with the guy being led away by the cops in the photo. The two men were in cahoots. One captured, while the other slipped by. He happened to end up in front of the newspaper photographer's lens. Unless it was intentional. Like he was showboating, rubbing it in the public's face how he got away. Which meant Leonard had gotten himself mixed up with some bad people. Real criminals. Since a casino was involved, perhaps Leonard had a secret gambling addiction. Owed the wrong people money.

I thought about Dr. Selnick, Leonard's therapist. The previous year, Leonard had told me he'd decided to see a shrink. He'd realized it was time he finally sorted out all the demons living in his head. The result of his tragic upbringing. He went twice a week. Monday nights and Thursday nights. He'd be gone for hours. He said the office was in Burlington, that he had to drive there and sometimes traffic was bad and the sessions were long. I didn't question him. He said Dr. Selnick was helping him, that after every session he walked away feeling optimistic. Like he was making progress. It seemed to me, however, that therapy was only causing Leonard to be more tired and moody. He slammed cupboards. He'd sleep in and have to stay late at work. He spent less and less time with me—he was too tired, too busy. He barely acknowledged Mother. I figured this was because the therapy was working. He and Dr. Selnick were driving right into the heart of his trauma and it was emotionally exhausting. He was getting better, but it would take some time. One step forward, two steps back. One night I asked him if it might be a good idea for my mother to see Dr. Selnick as well. Leonard said his therapist exclusively treated men, which I thought was odd. I asked him if there was another therapist in Selnick's office that could see Mother and he said there wasn't. I grew curious. Later that week, I searched for Dr. Selnick online and couldn't find anything. No trace of a men's-only therapist operating out of Burlington. I mentioned this to Leonard and he said Dr. Selnick didn't use computers. He was "old school," whatever that meant. I didn't bring it up again. I didn't want to press him. His relationship with his therapist was personal. But now, it seemed more likely that Leonard was lying. That maybe Mondays and Thursdays were when my husband drove down to Niagara Falls to gamble. It was during one of those "therapy nights" that Leonard got himself into trouble with the wrong people.

But who?

I hadn't read the article accompanying the *Metro* photograph. No idea what the man in cuffs had done. And I'd thrown out the rest of the paper. I needed another copy of Wednesday's *Metro*.

I called work. Luckily, Ken was still there. He reverted to his imperious attitude, complaining about my interruptions on the first night of a new Bank of America campaign, but I cut him down and told him to check the recycling bins for a copy of Wednesday's *Metro*. I told him there was a first aid article in there that I thought might be helpful in dealing with my mom, in case she'd fallen. He agreed to have a look and then bring it to Mother's. He said he'd leave right away.

The bus rolled by fields and storage facilities. A grey pond. A mattress outlet named Mattress Outlet. Too anxious to sleep, I got out my *Riders of Exley* notebook. Started sketching out a new scene: Mary Valentine storms into Stacy Maude Green's dorm and rips the blankets from her sleeping rival, slaps them on the floor. Delivers some earth-shattering monologue—I'd plug that in later. This would be my ending, I knew. Now I had to write the rest of the episode, find my way to this compelling climax. A whole new Mary Valentine. A force to be reckoned with. Maybe a parallel scene with Mary's horse chasing off a mean doppelganger horse with glowing red eyes.

We reached the outskirts of Toronto. I thought about Leonard, how he'd hidden things from me. A secret life. How could I have been so oblivious? My relationship with Leonard wasn't perfect. While he was still alive, I'd tried not to think about the little problems in our marriage. And they *were* little, insignificant problems, really. After he died, those miniscule issues faded from my mind completely. It was hard not to imagine Leonard as the ideal man and our marriage as a blissful paradise. It kind of was like that in the beginning, actually. When we first started dating. We'd meet for nice dinners or take romantic walks through Mimico. We had these deep conversations about life and TV shows. We'd smooch on park benches, even if the park was crowded with people. We'd go back to his apartment after a nice meal at Kelsey's, drink a glass of wine, and then make love on his futon. I thought about him while I was at work, and he said he thought about me at his work too.

Two months in, Leonard proposed. He didn't have a ring—it was a spontaneous thing. We were walking through High Park and came across the free zoo. I remember I was cold. It was December and I hadn't worn a heavy enough coat. I was complaining but Leonard didn't seem to mind. He was ecstatic. He loved all the animals and would talk to each one as if they were old friends. "You're so beautiful," he'd say to a peacock, "and you know it too!" I wasn't saying much that afternoon, except to whine about the cold or ask when we could leave.

Leonard was inspired, despite my grumpy attitude. He saw through all that and knew I had a good mood inside me, waiting just around the corner. We were standing in front of the buffalo pen, watching a buffalo eat grass. Leonard turned to me. He was staring at me. I idly kicked at the ground with the toe of my shoe. I wasn't paying attention to any of the animals. Then Leonard got down on one knee.

"I love you, Colleen," he said. "I don't want to be with anyone else. I only want days like this. I only want you. Let's get married."

I was shocked. I wasn't sure what to say. A family was standing at the buffalo fence near us and it felt like they were watching and listening in for my response. While I was thinking of something to say, the buffalo started throwing up. You could smell it. The watery vomit poured out of the buffalo like a pipe had burst. Leonard started laughing. I started laughing too. I was confused. Somewhere in there, I said yes. Later that week, we went down to a pawn shop and picked out rings. We married at City Hall the following month. Mother was our witness.

Things changed after we got married. Gradually. Leonard and I didn't go out so much anymore. He moved in with Mother and me and we stuck around the house. Made meals at home to save money. Watched sitcoms and talk shows. Leonard would play computer games while I worked on my screenplays in the kitchen. Within a year of living together, we'd transitioned into roommates. Sex became less and less frequent. We often ate dinner at different times. Leonard started working more. He was always exhausted. He'd work and sleep and drive to therapy, and I would just work and write scripts. We didn't really talk to each other; not the way we'd talked before, anyway. Practical discussions. What do we do about the raccoons, and so on. We lived parallel lives that rarely intersected. If only we had known that those would be our final months together.

Things were never *bad* though. Leonard wasn't cruel. We rarely fought. Almost never. Overall, our interactions could be described as pleasant. They just weren't perfect. We were figuring it out, like any other couple.

I taxied from the bus station to Mimico. All the lights were off at the house. The sky black. A *Metro* newspaper sat on the front steps—Ken had stopped by. Why hadn't he called? I went inside and shouted for Mother. No answer. The place was completely dark.

I began moving from room to room, turning on lights, calling out. A box of frozen pizza pockets was left out on the kitchen counter. A broom in the middle of the floor, for some reason. In the living room, the blankets and sheets from Mother's bed were piled on the sofa. The schedule I'd made for her sat on the coffee table, where I'd left it.

I heard a cough coming from the bathroom.

"Mother?"

Something shuffled around inside the bathroom, then silence. My heart pounded in my throat. I picked up the broom from the kitchen floor and moved toward the bathroom door. It was shut. No light under the door crack.

"Hello? Mother, are you in there?"

A loud sobbing echoed from inside.

I opened the door and turned on the light. Mother was huddled in the empty tub, head between her knees. She clutched a closed umbrella with both hands.

"Mother? What happened?"

"I'm so sorry, dear," she said, rocking back and forth.

I helped Mother out of the tub, led her over to the couch, and brewed her a cup of lemon tea. She eventually stopped crying and told me what had happened. Her new anxiety medication had knocked her out and she'd slept through all my calls. She still felt incredibly drowsy. We agreed to call her doctor the next day and see about cutting her dosage in half.

"What were you doing in the bathtub with the lights off?" I asked.

"That must have frightened you half to death, didn't it? I feel terrible, honey."

"It's okay. But what happened?"

"Maybe I was dreaming or maybe it was the medication. But I swear it was real. I woke up to someone pounding on the front door. Then the back door. It was so loud. It was a man. He shouted my name. It sounded like a maniac who wanted inside so he could pulverize me. I hid in the bathroom. He kept pounding and shouting things at me."

"That was my supervisor, Ken."

"Ken?"

"I sent him to check on you. I was concerned. He was making sure you were safe."

"He came all the way over here because of me? And I let him knock? I'm so embarrassed."

"I'm just happy you're safe."

"Maybe I should send him an apology letter. With a gift card. Can you get me his address?"

"You don't need to do that."

"Shopper's Drug Mart. There's something for everyone there. Would Ken enjoy a Shopper's Drug Mart gift card? Oh, but it will have to do."

Mother soon fell asleep. It was late and I'd had a long day, but I was riled up. I made toast. While I was eating, an email came in from Ken. He explained that he'd stopped by but had forgotten to write down my phone number to relay the info. He said he didn't talk to my mother, but he saw all the lights in the house go off, one by one, once he started knocking, so she was probably okay. He ended his message ominously: "We'll talk about your behaviour and future with the company on Monday."

I remembered the *Metro* on my front steps. I retrieved it, opened it up on the kitchen counter. Ken had pulled my own copy from the recycling bin, the relevant page torn out.

I went into my room, climbed into bed. Closed my eyes. And then I pictured Patti lying alone in the Captain's Inn. My empty bed sitting there cold, next to hers. It reminded me of nights on The Farm, when I'd often imagine my empty bed back at home and what Mother would think looking at it. If she was worried about me. But no, I'd correct myself, Mother doesn't care about me. The people here do, Woodbine does. Only they understand me.

Looking back, it was hard to accept that the person thinking those things was me. Poor Mother. Poor Patti. I was awake for hours.

I called Patti first thing in the morning, hoping to apologize. She didn't pick up. No one ever picks up for me. Phones don't work like that anymore. I'd try again later.

Mother was still asleep. I tiptoed around the kitchen, made coffee. Then turned on my laptop. I decided I'd search online for the story of the arrest at Fallsview. It took ten minutes of typing different combinations of words like "Fallsview," "crime," and "busted" into Google before I found an account of what had happened in the *Niagara Advance*. The accompanying picture was different—no guests from Leonard's funeral posing as employees. Just a stock photo of yellow police tape. The *Metro* article I'd originally seen wasn't online, or at least I couldn't find it. I sipped my coffee, scrolled through.

The cops had arrested one man: a Russian "tourist." He'd cheated the slot machines. There were other operatives involved and the cops were investigating. *Other operatives.* I wondered if Leonard was one of these. Probably not. The man from his funeral though. Maybe Leonard owed money to a Russian scam artist.

I found another article that went into more detail about the crime. It said that the casino's security team had noticed the Russian following an odd pattern. He only played older machines, which they later discovered were all manufactured by the same Australian company. He moved between *Betty Bumblebee, Space Jewels, Race to Rio, Farm Friends,* etc. No unusual payouts at first—he just walked from machine to machine, winning a little, losing a little. Basically evening out. Then he went outside onto one of Fallsview's smoking balconies for about an hour. Stared at his phone the entire time.

When the Russian came back in, he returned to the same old Australian machines. This time around, his payouts were much bigger and much more frequent. As if his luck had increased dramatically during his intermission on the balcony. He racked up nearly $8,000 in less than an hour.

Turns out, the "tourist" had kept his phone in his breast pocket during his initial rounds of the slot machines. He was streaming video of his activities over Skype to operatives back in Moscow. These operatives were figuring out each machine's unique system of "random" number generation. Apparently, these calculations are never truly random but rely on the internal mechanism of the machines—like their clock, for example. The Russians watching the tourist's Skype stream had the same old Australian machines in their possession back home. After gambling was outlawed in Russia in 2009, casinos sold off their slot machines at dramatically discounted prices, and criminals like the tourist and his pals bought them up and studied them until they cracked their systems of "randomness." The Russians watching over Skype quickly calculated the system for each machine, then created a custom timer unique to each console that would buzz his phone whenever it would be "lucky" to hit the spin button. There were Russians at casinos all over the world running the same scam.

I had to read the article three times before I understood the basics of what had gone down. I'm still not sure I really grasp the whole thing. But the takeaway is that a Russian crime syndicate of some notoriety flew a team of gamblers around from casino to casino, racking up unusually high slot machine payouts, and poor Leonard might have been mixed up in this somehow. One of these thugs might have killed my husband and dropped him in the bog. That's what these people do. There are stories in the news every week about bodies found in bogs, rivers, and gravel pits. It's organized crime every time.

I shut my laptop. Took a long shower. Mother's umbrella was still in there—I kicked it around the tub as I washed my hair. I had new information, but I wasn't sure what to do with it. I still needed to find the man in the vest. Which, if he didn't really work at the casino, might be impossible.

I towelled off. Ate a banana pudding. Tried ringing Patti again. Still no answer. Mother was still asleep. I logged onto Leonard's computer and opened *Reindeer Island*.

Heartsong galloped through the bluffs along the western edge of the Moroni Sands Golf Club. A mid-morning haze clung to the tall grass. On the horizon, atop the ridge separating Moroni Sands from the vast Joseph Smith Forest, stood a reindeer.

Don't run off, I thought. Stay right there.

Heartsong made a beeline for the ridge. I couldn't tell if it was Bonsai, or some other reindeer. Hopefully they would want to solve a puzzle or even just explore the island with me.

Heartsong reached the bottom of the ridge and looked up at the reindeer. It wasn't Bonsai. Their fur was too dark. They didn't have a name—usually, the player's username floated above the reindeer in a yellow font. Heartsong stamped his right hoof twice. No response.

Once Heartsong climbed the ridge, I realized it wasn't another player. It was a reindeer statue. Its stone legs were fixed to a rectangular stone base. There were two other stone bases, on either side of the statue. Heartsong walked onto one of the empty bases and positioned himself just like the statue, facing out over the golf course. One of the statue's eyes lit up. If another reindeer stood on the other empty base, the other eye would light up and something would happen. But there were no other reindeer. Nothing happened.

Heartsong stepped off the base and walked into the forest. I'd keep exploring. Mother would wake soon. I heard something in my earbuds. A crack. Heartsong turned around. A silver reindeer was running through the trees, back toward the top of the ridge. Bonsai. He had been following me.

Heartsong exited the forest and stood atop the ridge. Bonsai was already down on the golf course, fleeing. I pressed the shift key, which made the reindeer gallop.

Heartsong pursued Bonsai across the greens and down the path leading back to Main Pool. They crossed the sand dunes to the beach and began moving along the coast, heading north, digital sand flying across the screen in their wake. They galloped at a steady pace. The sun slowly setting over the water, the reindeers' shadows lengthening along the beach. Bonsai left the beach and ran into a thicket of bushes.

Emerging from the bushes, Heartsong found himself among rows of trees in perfect alignment. Red fruit scattered along the ground. An apple orchard. Bonsai was stopped up ahead, waiting. Heartsong trotted up and stood face to face with Bonsai again.

Heartsong stamped a right hoof, then left. Paced around Bonsai in a circle. No response. Soon, Bonsai's head dropped down and little Zs began to float out of his mouth.

Mother eventually woke up and we decided to bus down to IKEA for lunch. IKEA is our favourite restaurant. It's cafeteria style, so you can pay before you eat and then enjoy your food without worrying about the damn cheque the whole time. They have great dessert selections and it's convenient if you need a new office chair or knife block. We both ordered the meatball meal, which we always order. I had a raspberry soda and Mother had chocolate milk. The dining area was crowded with strollers, young couples, and a big group of men with white paint all over their jeans and boots. Mother was telling me about a documentary she saw on TV while I was away in Niagara about a pizza delivery boy who put poison in the pizzas. I was half listening, half thinking about what I should do about Niagara Falls. Maybe I could somehow go back and talk to the security team at Fallsview. They could help me smoke the Metro Man out of hiding. And then Mother stopped talking mid-sentence. I looked up from my meatball meal and Mother leaned toward me.

"That's him," she said. "The big man who stopped by the house while you were gone and asked about you." She gestured with her fork, and I looked to my left.

There was Patti's husband, Dougie, staring at me.

Dougie looked angry. He was standing in the food line holding a plastic tray and the tray was bent in the middle like he was trying to snap it in two with his grip. He pushed past an elderly couple, nearly knocking them over, and stomped over to our table.

"Patti's friend," he said. "You're that Colleen."

"How do you do, Dougie?" I was surprised he'd recognized me. I'd only met him once before, the previous summer, when he'd picked Patti up from our office barbeque and reluctantly drove me home too. I started wiping my hands with a napkin in case he wanted to shake hands, even though I was using a fork and had clean hands.

"That goddamn liar!" Dougie said. Other diners looked over at our table. "She told me she was going to Niagara Falls with you for the weekend."

"I had to come back—"

"Did you know about this? Are you goddamn covering for Patti?" He threw his tray onto the floor. A young cashier came out from behind his till, but then just stood there watching us.

"Dougie, calm down. I was absolutely with your wife in Niagara Falls. We went to the casino. We're staying at the Captain's Inn. I had to come—"

"Liar! You're covering. Goddamnit, who is she with? Someone from work? Is it goddamn Craig?"

Dougie reached down and plucked two meatballs from Mother's plate and shoved them into his mouth. There was red sauce all over his hand and chin. He stared at Mother while he chewed. Mother looked down at her chest.

"Excuse me?" I stood up. My chair fell over backward and clattered against the floor. I stuck my finger in Dougie's greasy face. "I was with your wife, who is a good, kind woman, by the way, and I had to come back because my mother needed me."

"If you think I'm—"

"You're going to apologize to my mother. And then you're going to march right over to that counter and buy her a new plate of meatballs."

"Please, don't worry about that," Mother said, her eyes still cast down at her chest, her voice trembling.

"Oh, fuck off," Dougie said. He walked closer to me so we were standing toe to toe. I didn't budge. "And fuck your meatballs. You're a liar and I know Patti's fucking around on me. I'm not stupid. So guess what?"

"Yeah, what?" I squinted my eyes all mean at Dougie.

"I'm heading down there right now. Captain's Inn, you said? You better pray to Jesus she's on the goddamn register and you better pray to Jesus she's not in there with Craig or some other prick. Because if I find out you're covering for Patti, the second I'm done dealing with her, I'm coming for you."

We held our stare for a few seconds. The restaurant was silent. Then Dougie stormed off. I couldn't think of anything to say in return, so I watched him disappear into the crowd of people huddled apprehensively by the restaurant entrance unsure of what was going on and if it was okay to enter. I turned to Mother. She looked up at me.

"I'm sorry," she said.

Patti wasn't answering her phone. I tried her three times, hoping to warn her about Dougie. Would he really drive down there? I wondered. He'd likely call instead and have it out with her on the phone. Which was why I couldn't get through to her. Still, I thought I should let her know what was happening in case Dougie hadn't called and she wasn't answering because she was mad at me for leaving.

I sent Patti a text: *Ran into Dougie and he thinks you're cheating because I'm here and he's driving to NF now. I'm sorry. I tried to explain but he was so angry.*

Mother and I were still working our way through our meatball meals, but the vibe was uncomfortable now. People were staring at us, or it felt like they were. We took our drinks and left our half-eaten meals on the table. As we were walking out, my phone rang.

It was Patti. She was frantic. Her voice was pitched a little higher and there was all this muffled breathing into the phone, like she was rushing around outside.

"Does he know what hotel?" Patti said. "Did you tell him?"

"Yes, he knows. But didn't you already tell him where we were staying?"

"No. I didn't. This is really none of your business, but Dougie and I had a fight. I wasn't just coming with you to Niagara Falls for a vacation. I needed to get away from him."

"What do you mean?"

"Exactly what I fucking said. I needed to get away from Dougie. We had a fight. Do you know what I did today, Colleen? I applied for serving jobs here in town. I have an interview at IHOP tomorrow morning."

"IHOP? Why would you do that?"

"Because I'm done with Dougie. I'm here now. But maybe that's all ruined because you abandoned me and then you went and told Dougie where I'm staying. What am I going to do?"

"Did he hit you? I noticed you have a bruise."

"That's none of your goddamn business. Shit. I need to get out of here. And I can't go back to Toronto."

"Stay there, Patti. I'm coming back. I'll catch the next bus and meet you somewhere. Check out of the Captain right away and park your car somewhere else. Put it in the underground lot at the casino, okay? Then find another hotel for us. I'll text you when I'm on the road."

"You're really coming back?"

"Of course. I'm sorry I left you, but I'll be there soon."

I looked over at Mother. We were in the parking lot now, walking toward the bus stop. She was staring straight ahead as if she wasn't listening in, but her eyes looked worried. I was leaving her again.

11

I took a Greyhound back to Niagara Falls. I brought a flashlight and dark clothes with me this time. Leonard's laptop, too, in case I needed to do research. I could have driven Leonard's car, but I wasn't ready. It still sat in our driveway. The last person to drive it was Leonard—the police had it towed from Morrison Bog to Mimico. The thought of sitting in Leonard's seat with my hands on his steering wheel gave me this uneasy feeling, like I'd die too.

Mother promised to follow the schedule from now on, and I promised not to freak out if she didn't answer my calls right away—she was likely sleeping. As soon as she woke up, she'd call me back and confirm that she was still breathing. It wasn't an ideal situation, but I had to go. Patti needed me. And I wasn't through investigating Leonard's death.

I borrowed Mother's credit card in case of an emergency. I hadn't quite reached the limit on my own card yet, but I felt safer having a backup. The debt I was accruing with these trips would become a problem for me, but it would become a problem for me later. I accepted this inevitability. For now, there was work to do.

I sat next to the window and kept my eyes on the road for Dougie, as if I'd see him pass by, his arm protruding from the driver's window, his fist shaking furiously. But then I remembered that Patti had their car with her. They didn't have a second vehicle. Which got me wondering how Dougie was planning to get to Niagara Falls. Was he also taking the bus? Was he on *my* bus? Was he sitting in the seat behind me, staring at the back of my head, seething with rage? Unlikely, but I still slunk down in my seat.

Halfway to Niagara Falls, I had a sneezing fit. My seatmate, an old woman with cat hair on her sleeves, said, "God bless you" after the first sneeze. Then she said it after the second sneeze, and again after the third.

"This will likely go on for a bit," I said. "I'm so sorry. You don't have to keep saying 'God bless you.'"

"But I like saying it," she said. "I hope you sneeze all the way to the bus depot!"

I sneezed.

"God bless you."

I got into one of the taxis waiting at the station and gave the driver the name of the hotel Patti had texted to me earlier, the Queen Fallsview. We drove toward the falls. I noted that Patti's car wasn't in the lot as we passed by the Captain's Inn, nor was Patti's fuming husband.

The cab continued to the main strip and pulled up directly across from the Fallsview Casino.

"Excuse me," I said to the driver, "I said the *Queen* Fallsview. It's a hotel."

"On your right, miss," he said.

I looked out the passenger side and there it was, printed on the glass of the front doors in gold cursive: the Queen Fallsview. A man in an old-fashioned suit and cap stood there, hands clasped behind his back. I looked up. The building was enormous. And fancy as hell. Right across the street from the casino. If your room was high up enough, you'd be able to look out your window and see the falls. It looked expensive and I was angry with Patti for picking such an extravagant place, but I also couldn't wait to get inside. I forgot about the taxi fare and ran out onto the sidewalk. The driver had to honk his horn so I'd come back and pay.

The lobby was like a classy aircraft hangar with staircases surrounding a fountain and potted ferns everywhere. Gold plaques on the wall. The floor probably wasn't marble but it was made to look like marble. I smelled cinnamon buns and looked up and saw that there was an actual Cinnabon kiosk in the hotel, on the second-floor atrium. Guests could zip down in their pajamas for a delicious Cinnabon breakfast.

I waited with two sweaty, sunburnt families by the four elevators that ascended the heights of the Queen Fallsview. Patti was on the thirty-fourth floor anticipating my arrival. It was reckless for her to pick such a swanky place, but it also showed her refined taste. The Captain's Inn, the hotel I'd picked, didn't have an elevator. It didn't even have clean floors.

When I got to our room, I knocked and knocked but Patti didn't answer. Then I got a text from Patti: *Hold on I'm in the bath.*

I sat on the carpet in the hallway and waited. I noticed a little boy leaning from a doorway down the hall, staring at me. He wore an eye patch. A little villain. I waved at the boy, he popped back inside his room.

Patti answered the door in a fluffy white robe and let me into the suite. That's the kind of room it was—you wouldn't even stoop to call it a room because it was a *suite*. Spacious, clean, and the furniture matched. No smudge marks on the bathroom mirror. A window stretched from floor to ceiling on the far side of the room, and you could see the falls. I pressed my face to the glass and looked out in awe.

"Quite a view, right?" Patti said.

"It's majestic," I said.

We weren't saying much. Patti sat at the end of one of the two beds, clipping her nails onto the carpet. I remained by the window, admiring the view. I wanted to ask Patti about her husband and what had happened, but I wasn't sure if it was appropriate. Like perhaps I should wait until she wanted to talk about it. I was also a little peeved that she hadn't asked about Mother. I mean, I fled in a panic because my mom wasn't answering the phone and I expected Patti to at least mention this in some small way.

Patti finished with her nails, flicked on the TV, and lay back in her bed. She changed channels and then settled on a show about a serial killer who mailed his victims' body parts to the White House. I sat down on the unoccupied bed and watched the program. The killer spent his formative years living on a boat and they showed pictures of the boat's interior. It looked warm and cozy. There was a clock on the wall that Mother also had in her room, with birds in place of the numbers.

When the show ended, Patti turned off the TV and we sat in silence for a few minutes. Then Patti turned to me.

"Do you want to get an apartment with me?" she asked.

"What do you mean?"

"An apartment. It's a thing in a building where people live."

"I don't understand. I already live somewhere."

"You want to live with your mommy forever? Christ, Colleen. Maybe it's time to grow up. Anyway, Toronto is old news. Niagara Falls is where we should be now. Do you want to move in with me? I can probably get you an interview at IHOP too."

"You want to live in Niagara Falls?"

"Hell yes, I do. Niagara Falls is amazing. It's got that border town energy. We can work at IHOP, go to the casino. It's got everything."

"That sounds nice and all, but I've got Mother."

"Just think about it. Can you think about it? Let's go downstairs and get a drink."

The Queen Fallsview had its own cocktail lounge on the main floor, across from the entrance to the pool. You could smell the pool chemicals. Four stools at the bar and four small tables. The area was cordoned off by plastic posts with retractable bands like they have at the bank. We sat at one of the tables. Patti said the bartender looked like Robert Stack and I laughed, even though I don't know who Robert Stack is.

It was nice to reunite with Patti on good terms and have mojitos and laugh, but I wanted to go off on my own. I knew I only had so much time to look into Leonard's death. I was heading back to Mimico and Mother the next day. I needed a reason to sneak off so I could walk over to the casino and talk to the security guards.

"I might take a walk after this drink," I said. "I need to clear my head. Is that okay?"

"Sure. I'll come with."

"Oh, good. But maybe I should go by myself this time. I'll keep an eye out for Dougie."

"No, it's fine. Where do you wanna go? We should check out Clifton Hill. Apparently there's an upside-down house and I want some Dippin' Dots."

"Actually, now that I think about it, I should rest. I'm pretty tired from the ride down. You go ahead. I'll take a little nap."

"I could nap. We can get Dippin' Dots after."

"Hmm. Yeah, okay."

It was hopeless, I realized. I'd have to find another opening to strike off on my own. And then Patti crossed her arms in this dramatic fashion and gave me a look. She raised her eyebrows, scrunched her mouth. Her eyes focused in on me like a preda-tor bird.

"What?" I asked.

"You're hiding something."

"Don't be ridiculous. What would I be hiding?"

"You tell me."

"I'm not hiding *any*thing."

"Okay."

"I'm really not."

"Okay."

She continued to stare at me. I kept picking up my mojito and sipping it, much too frequently. She knew something was up. I couldn't take it.

"I'm not hiding anything!" I slapped the table.

"Of course."

"Fine." I came clean. I told her everything.

I told her about the man from Leonard's funeral, how he kept to himself and then lied about working at the plastics plant. I told her about finding him again in the *Metro* paper—I showed Patti the clipping. Then I told her that I'd presented the clipping to two bartenders at Fallsview who said they'd never seen the man in the vest before. I told her about the Russians and their slot machine scam. Patti leaned in close, her mouth open, eyes darting around. She loved it, I could tell. She all but squealed with delight. It felt good to unburden myself. Like I'd been lugging around a grocery bag stuffed with heavy spaghetti sauce jars and now Patti was holding one of the bag's handles and we were walking the jars home together.

"Why didn't you tell me any of this?" Patti said. "Do you think Leonard was in the Mafia or something? Have you ever heard him speak Russian?"

"I don't know. I don't think so."

"I bet that he hid a stash of gambling money somewhere. In the bog! Colleen, the bog!"

Maybe it was a mistake telling Patti what I was up to, I thought. But it was already done—I'd told her. And anyway, Mother used to say that when you regret doing something it's because you can only see the short-term results and all the good stuff would come later. Like if you go running and you get a cramp. Maybe you regret running because of the cramp, but then later you have strong legs and fun memories of running by the lake. Patti might help out with the investigation.

"What's the next step?" Patti set her now empty mojito glass on the table and leaned back in her chair.

"I was going to talk to security at the casino."

"I'll go get changed."

12

We'd just stepped out into the street when Patti's phone buzzed. It was Dougie. Patti got spooked and ran back inside—she didn't answer the call. She felt like her husband was watching her from somewhere, because he'd called the second she left the hotel. I went out onto the sidewalk and looked around, but I didn't see Dougie anywhere. Patti wasn't convinced. She wanted to go back up to the room. I'd have to go about the mission alone. I promised Patti I'd keep her updated via text and then I went outside and walked over to Fallsview.

Once inside the casino, I walked around the perimeter of the room until I found a security guard. I approached her slowly, rehearsing my little spiel inside my head one last time.

"Excuse me," I said. The security guard raised her eyebrows. "My name is Annie Hart. I am looking to speak with the head of security. I have information about the Russian scam artist who was arrested here last week."

"That's a police matter," the security guard said.

"Yes, but I thought I should come to you first. And then you can see if the police need to be involved."

"Okay. The police need to be involved."

"But can't I deal with your team initially? It has to do with someone posing as a Fallsview employee. An imposter. That's a Fallsview issue."

"Fine, what information do you have?"

"I'd really rather speak with the head of security."

The security guard glared at me. I smiled back.

The security guard led me through a locked door, down a narrow hallway, and into a small office. A bald man sat behind a desk, yelling into a phone. He was yelling in French. Behind him, a glass window looked into another room with another bald man at a desk. This other bald man's desk was covered with computers and wires and binders. Above the desk, eight TV screens were mounted to the wall, displaying security camera footage.

"Wait here," the security guard said. She leaned into the room with the TV screens and said something to the man at the desk. They talked for a minute and the security guard came out and pointed at me.

"Make this quick," she said.

The bald man inside the TV room looked annoyed. He wore a leather jacket over his security uniform, which seemed too small for his large frame. It squeaked as he leaned back in his chair. The room smelled like bad breath.

"You have information about the arrest last week?" he asked.

"Yes," I said. I took the *Metro* clipping from my pocket and handed it to him.

"That's the suspect, yes."

"Okay," I said. "But do you see the man in the background? Wearing the Fallsview vest? I think he might be involved somehow. I don't think he really works for the casino."

The bald man squinted at the clipping, rubbed his chin. The ends of his fingers were orange, and now he had orange smudges on his face.

"Close the door," the bald man said.

I closed it.

"This is from the paper?" he continued.

"Yes, sir. The Toronto *Metro*."

"You're from Toronto?"

"Yes, sir."

"What's your name, miss?"

"Annie. Annie Hart."

"Annie Hart. How do you know this man in the photo?"

"I don't."

"Okay. And what makes you think he doesn't work at Fallsview?"

"I spoke to one of your bartenders and—"

"Bartenders? Annie, why were you talking to the bartenders in the first place? Why are you here? What does this Russian criminal have to do with you?"

"I'm a concerned citizen."

"A concerned citizen. Well, Annie, I thank you for your concern, but I'm very busy here. The police are investigating the case and I can assure you they're investigating it thoroughly. I don't know what bartender you were talking to, but I know the man in the photo and he was definitely a Fallsview employee. Okay?"

"*Was?* Who is he? Does he not work here anymore?"

"You know, I don't feel comfortable giving that information out. I don't know who you are. The important thing is that he worked here and so your imposter theory doesn't quite pan out. Now please, we're busy here. Thank you for your time."

The bald man swivelled in his chair, back to his desk. He opened up a newspaper and turned to the horoscopes page. I waited for a second, thinking he would hand back my *Metro* clipping, but he didn't.

Back on the casino floor, I texted Patti: *Talked to security, apparently the guy does work here, didn't get a name. Should I look for him?*

Patti responded: *We'll look later, I'm hungry. Let's hit up Jimmy B again.*

On first glance, I didn't think anything of the man with the round glasses. I saw him reflected in one of the mirrors on the ceiling. He was walking behind me as I made my way through the casino, toward the exit. Short blond hair, blue bomber jacket, and thick, perfectly round glasses.

On my way out, however, I passed the washroom and realized I needed to pee. When I left the washroom, I saw the man again. He was standing at the end of a row of slot machines, looking at his phone. Again, I didn't think anything of it. I noticed him the way I notice lots of people. He had interesting glasses. I walked on.

I was nearing the entrance when I happened to look up at another ceiling mirror. The man was behind me again. The thought crossed my mind that he might be following me. Probably just paranoia, what with all that had happened in the last couple of days. Regardless, I decided to test him. I took a sharp left and walked down another row of slot machines, toward the table games.

I didn't see him at first. I made my way past the table games, through a corridor of dollar slots, and up to the counter where you cash out your winnings. I stopped beside the counter and pretended to go through my purse. I looked up at the mirror—there was the man in the round glasses. Leaning against one of the dollar slots, looking at his phone again.

I pulled a tube of ChapStick from my purse and applied it, so it would look like I really did stop to go through my purse. I didn't want the man to know that I knew he was following me, if that was indeed what he was doing. Which meant I needed to justify my choice to weave through all the machines and tables to get to the cash-out counter. Then I noticed the sign on the wall, at the end of the counter: Smoking Patio. I walked over and went outside.

There was a beautiful view of the falls, but I wasn't interested in looking at the falls. I pulled out my phone. The low battery warning was on. I called Patti and kept my eye on the door to the patio.

"Where are you?" Patti said. "Mama needs a peppercorn burger, ASAP."

"Never mind that, something weird is happening over here. I think someone's following me."

"You're kidding. Really?"

"I saw this man walking behind me everywhere I went, so I took a weird route through the casino and he stayed on me."

"You think it's one of Dougie's friends?"

"I don't know. It could be. Or maybe it's someone connected to Fallsview security. Does Dougie have a friend with round glasses?"

"Round glasses? I don't think so. I mean, Dougie doesn't really have any friends."

"I'm not sure what to do. Should I confront him?"

"Oh God, no. Don't do that. He could be dangerous."

"Well, I can't lead him back to our hotel. Maybe I could go into a different hotel. You could come over and watch, see what he does. You could follow *him*."

"I guess I could do that. Jesus Christ. How do we do this?"

"Get over here. I'll come out the front entrance of the casino, where we came in yesterday. I'll call you when I'm about to walk out. Wait outside and see if he's still following me. I'll walk over to some other hotel and you follow him. See what he does. A man with round glasses. He has a blue jacket. Kind of tall."

"I'm putting on my shoes."

13

When I walked back in from the patio, the man in the round glasses was still leaning against the same dollar slot machine. He glanced up at me, then focused in on his phone again. I made my way toward the front entrance.

I called Patti.

"I'm outside," she said.

"Okay, I'm walking out into the atrium now," I said. I spoke quietly, in case the man was close behind. "You'll see me through the doors in a second. Just ignore me and watch the entrance. See if the man in the round glasses and blue jacket comes out."

"Alright. Okay, there you are."

Patti stood on the sidewalk just outside the doors. Taxis were lined up on the street next to her. She wore a green dress I'd never seen before, and she looked amazing. The sky was dark and the lights from the taxis gave Patti a sexy glow. I was worried she'd wave to me or smile at me too obviously, which could tip off whoever was following me, but she ignored me.

I followed the walkway down to the street and waited at the crosswalk.

"Anything?" I asked.

"Not yet. Blue jacket?"

"Yes. And round glasses."

"What colour hair? Oh wait . . . I think he's coming."

"Short blond hair?"

"I think so. Yes. Round glasses. He looks like one those perverts you see on the news. Okay, I better be quiet for a second."

"Okay."

I wanted to turn around, but I stared across the street. Patti was breathing into the phone. Several other pedestrians crowded around me. The walk signal came on and I crossed the road. The Queen Fallsview entrance stood just to my left, but I turned right and continued down the sidewalk, away from my hotel.

"He's walking your way," Patti said.

"Oh my God. Okay, keep your distance. I'll go into the next hotel. Tell me what he does."

"Alright. Are you scared?"

"Kind of. Yes, I am. Are you?"

"Same. This is fucked up, Colleen."

"I'm sorry. I shouldn't have—"

"He's staring at you!" Patti squealed. "Sorry, I should keep my voice down. He didn't hear me though. But he's waiting at the crosswalk and he's one-hundred percent watching you."

"Oh my God."

I walked past several restaurants, a Starbucks. I could see a Hilton sign up ahead on the next block.

"He's crossing the road," Patti said. "Okay. Hold on, I'm behind a van. Hold on. Okay, he's turning right. He's walking your way."

"Keep following. I'm going into the Hilton just up the street. Do you see it?"

"Yes. Good. Patti's coming, don't worry."

I kept a steady, normal walking pace. My instincts told me to bolt for the hotel, but I couldn't let the man in the round glasses know that I knew he was behind me. When I reached the Hilton, the automatic doors slid open and I walked inside.

A group of senior citizens crowded around the reception desk. They all wore jackets that said "Junie's Crew" on the backs. The receptionist's attention was absorbed, but I gave her a nod anyway and continued through the lobby.

"I'm inside," I said, once I got to the elevators and was sure no one was behind me. "Is he still following?"

I waited, but there was no answer.

"Patti?"

I looked at my phone—it was dead.

I called the elevator and one immediately opened behind me. I entered and pressed three, seven, and eight. I stared at my lifeless phone, holding the power button down. Nothing happened. I got off on the third floor.

I walked down the hall until I found a window overlooking the street. My side of the street wasn't visible. The opposite side was, but I couldn't see Patti or the man in the round glasses. Did he follow me into the hotel? He could check each floor, I thought. I took one last scan of the street and moved back down the hall until I found the ice machine room. I went inside and sat down on the ground beside the ice machine. It was nice and cool in there. The hum of the machine was soothing.

One thing was clear now: I was onto something. I'd come to Niagara Falls to investigate Leonard's death and my one lead in the case—the man in the *Metro*—seemed to be surrounded by suspicious activity. The bartender said he didn't think the man worked at the casino, which meant he wore the Fallsview uniform as a disguise. But the head of security said the man did, at least at some point, work there. And then someone followed me out of the casino and over to the Hilton.

I reached into the ice machine, plucked out two cubes, and put them in my mouth. Listened for footsteps in the hall. All was quiet. I wondered if my recent activities would make for an exciting *Riders of Exley* script. Maybe Mary Valentine's class could take a field trip to Niagara Falls. Hard to see why they'd choose this destination—I hadn't seen any horses around—but I could figure it out later.

I was thinking about what could happen in the episode, and I remembered the time my class went on a field trip to Medieval Times. I was held back a year, because I'd been away with the Citizens of Light and missed most of the tenth grade. I didn't really know anyone in my class. The other kids kept their distance. I think they'd heard what happened and didn't understand how to act around me. When we got to the restaurant, I decided to stay on the bus. I'm not sure what made me do that. I guess I just didn't want to be around my classmates. I didn't trust them. No one noticed my absence. Not even the driver. I listened to him argue with his wife over the phone, until he left too. I stared at the back of the seat in front of me and shivered in the cold. A few hours later, everyone returned to the bus and we drove back to the school. Nobody seemed to notice that I hadn't joined them in Medieval Times. When I got home, I told Mother that I'd watched a jousting tournament and ate a big steak dinner. I remember going to bed hungry that night.

Of course, a *Riders of Exley* episode based on that experience wouldn't be terribly exciting. Just sad. And when you're writing a spec script, you don't want to screw around with the format. You want to use the sets the show has on hand, not write in entirely new locations. This messed with the show's budget. Also, the producers want to hire writers who can work within the limitations of the show. They want to see that you have a unique, exciting voice, but that you can squeeze it into the world they've created. Perhaps Exley Riding School could host a carnival and Mary Valentine could go to a kid's casino on the premises, like in a big tent, and she'd spend the episode searching for a mysterious horse with a scar under its eye she saw in the school newsletter.

It was calming, thinking about the show. I chomped another ice cube. Normally I didn't mine my own life for story ideas. When I'd tried this in the past, the story always came out dull and depressing, and it ruined the fun of exploring my imagination. When I first started writing TV shows, I was seeing a therapist named Zeigland, and Zeigland encouraged me to write about my experiences on The Farm. I started working on an original script about a teenager who runs away and joins up with a cult. It wasn't any good. I mean, not that my other scripts are necessarily good, but at least they are fun to write. This cult script made me feel miserable. The title I came up with was *Cult*. When I finished it, I cut the script up into tiny pieces and ran the vacuum over it.

The funny thing—though maybe it's not funny at all—is that I would have had an easier time getting people to read the cult script. Because I actually was in a cult. Some of these producers would remember the story from the newspapers, and perhaps even recognize my name. One of the other teenagers who lived on The Farm with me, Lacy, wrote a book about the Citizens of Light and had it published. I never read it. I didn't want anything to do with that part of my past, and I certainly didn't want to build my dream career of writing TV shows on the foundations of something so terrible. I'd work for *Riders of Exley* or another show because the producers would decide that I was talented. Not because I'd lived in some ghoulish house with an insane person.

I wouldn't write about Niagara Falls, I decided. That would make me think about Leonard dying, and I didn't want to think about that. TV scripts were a way to escape the drearier aspects of reality. I'd write about Mary Valentine finding a book of spells in the latrine. She tries one of the spells and it makes her horse run faster. Or Mary takes swimming lessons and sees a family of ghosts who live at the bottom of the lake. Something fun like that.

The ice was starting to hurt my cheeks. I needed to get back to the Queen Fallsview and charge my phone. Patti was likely worried. And she could be in trouble too, I thought. The man in the round glasses could be inside the hotel, though, or posted out front, waiting for me to emerge. Maybe there was another exit. A backdoor. A secret alley that would take me right to my hotel undetected. I poked my head out of the ice room—all clear—and took the stairs back down to the main floor.

I emerged by the elevators. A woman waited with her daughter. The daughter wore water wings and she was crying.

"My arms are squeaking," the girl said. "I hate it."

I walked down the hall toward the back of the building. I passed by the pool room. I could hear children screaming through the door. A wet sock sat in the middle of the hallway. I found another stairwell at the end of the hall. Inside, a door with an exit sign hanging above. I opened it and stepped out.

I was standing in some kind of loading area. A man and a woman in chef's clothes were smoking beside another door. They were staring at me. I smiled back at them, a big idiotic grin. They both narrowed their eyes, but they didn't say anything. The man in the round glasses was nowhere in sight. An alleyway stretched along the back side of the building. I followed it in the direction of the Queen Fallsview, until I reached another alley that led along the western edge of the Hilton to the main street. When I got to the end of that alley, I poked my head out and searched around for the man in the round glasses. I must have looked insane, peering around the corner like a paranoid bird, but the man wasn't there. I walked as fast as I could manage down the sidewalk, jostling groups of slow tourists, until the sliding doors of the Queen Fallsview popped open and I slipped inside.

Patti wasn't in the room. I plugged in my phone and watched the battery icon flash. It would take a few minutes of charging before I could use it. I paced around the carpet.

My phone came to life and I saw that I had three missed calls from Patti, as well as several texts:

Colleen???

Answer your goddamn phone!!!

Okay well the guy got into a car and I'm in a cab following him.
This is insane. Answer your phone!

Hellooooo

The last text was sent twenty minutes earlier. I called Patti—
no answer.

My stomach was in knots. I knelt on the carpet, staring at my
phone, waiting for something to happen. Like a cat watching a dead
bug. The only thing that existed for me in that moment was my
phone, and so when Patti walked in the door, I screamed. I jumped
forward and hit my head against the wall. Patti screamed too.

She was still holding the door open and a man from a neigh-
bouring room appeared behind her. He asked us if everything was
alright.

"I heard shouts," the man said. His face was completely sunburnt. It was painful to look at.

"We're fine, thanks," Patti said. "Just startled each other."

"I thought there might have been an attacker," the man said.
He looked down at me on the carpet, where I lay rubbing my sore
head. "Just so you know, if you guys have any problems, come
knock on my door. I'm right across the hall. I'm actually trained
in combat."

"We'll keep that in mind," Patti said.

"In fact, if you two want a defense lesson I can bring my
brother over. He's trained in combat too. We can run through
some scenarios."

"Thanks, but we'll pass."

The man looked heartbroken as Patti closed the door on him.

Patti and I sat on our beds and exchanged stories. I told her that
my phone had died once I was inside the Hilton and that I decided
to sneak around the back alley to return to our hotel.

"What happened with the guy?" I asked. "You went after him in a cab?"

"He followed you into the Hilton. I was so scared. I was going to go in and make sure you were alright, but then the man came right back outside and phoned someone," Patti said. "Then he just stood there for a while. In front of the Starbucks. I noticed that our call had dropped and I tried you back a few times, but obviously that didn't work. A few minutes later, a black car pulled up to the curb and the man got in. I was on the other side of the street and there were all these taxis lined up in front of me. The black car pulled a U-turn and then waited at the crosswalk. I wasn't sure what to do. I tried calling you again. And then I got into one of the taxis and told the driver to pull up behind the black car."

"Like on one of those shows," I said.

"It was exactly like that, like on a show. I passed the driver a twenty and told him to follow the black car. But to keep a safe distance. I said my husband was in the black car and that I wanted to surprise him."

"So where did the black car go?"

"A haunted house."

"What do you mean?"

"I mean a haunted house. Like on Halloween. We were in Clifton Hill. It was like a carnival. There were rides and ice cream stands, this giant Frankenstein. We have to go back there. Anyway, the black car parked on a side street. The man in the round glasses and another man, the driver of the black car, got out. I followed them on foot. They walked into Clifton Hill and then went into a haunted house. The sign out front said Mayhem Manor. They used a key to go inside."

"Mayhem Manor?"

"There were a lot of people walking around and going into the different fun houses, so it was weird that they had to use a key to go in. I guess the man who was following you works there. I waited a few minutes and then went up to the door. There was a notice posted saying Mayhem Manor was closed for renovations. Then I got another cab and came back here."

"I was followed by a haunted house operator?"

"I guess so."

"We have to go back there," I said. "Tomorrow morning, before we head home."

"I'm not going home," Patti said. "I have my IHOP interview tomorrow, remember?"

"You're actually staying here?"

"I live here now, Colleen. Once I get the job, I'm looking for an apartment. I think you should stay too."

"I can't."

"Don't you want to find out what happened to Leonard? What these guys are up to?"

"Well, yes, but—"

"My interview's at ten. We'll go over to Mayhem Manor afterward."

14

We ate cinnamon buns from the lobby Cinnabon on our beds, watching *Dateline*. The episode was about a retired cop who broke into homes in the middle of the night and took pictures of people sleeping. He made paintings of the pictures and sold them on Etsy. They weren't very good, but the show's host said people bought them.

"Do you think you can still buy his paintings?" Patti asked.

"I don't know. He's locked up now, isn't he?"

"I bet he can still use his Etsy. They have internet in the prison library. He can use the money he makes from Etsy in the commissary. I'm getting one of those paintings for my new apartment. With my first IHOP cheque."

Patti fell asleep. I turned the TV off. I couldn't stomach *Dateline* alone, in the dark. I went into the washroom and called Mother. She'd been watching *Dateline* too, but a different episode. She said that she missed me but that she was doing fine. Actually, she said, it was kind of fun having the place to herself. She'd dusted off her old harmonica and played a few bars. She had a bath with the door open.

"Have a nice last day in Niagara Falls, sweetie," she said, yawning. "I can't wait to see you tomorrow night. I found one of the good Costco lasagnas in the freezer. It was behind the popsicles. We can have that and watch a DVD."

We said goodnight and I moved back to my bed. I wasn't ready to leave Niagara Falls. It really felt like I was getting somewhere with my investigation. I needed more time. But I still had the morning and part of the afternoon to find more information. I'd get up early and work twice as hard. Check out that haunted house. Patti was snoring. She sounded like one of those over-bred dogs that can't breathe properly. I wasn't quite sleepy yet. I fired up Leonard's laptop and opened *Reindeer Island*.

Heartsong stood on the expansive seaside patio of the Spencer W. Kimball Grill. Waves crashed into the beach and the low morning sun cast a wide band of shimmering light across the water. Seagulls called out to each other in the distance, in my earbuds.

I decided to visit the tortoise enclosure over by Cumorah Hill. If you stamped the ground in front of them, they did a little dance for you. Heartsong left the restaurant patio and trotted across the parking lot toward Moroni Sands—the fastest route to Cumorah Hill was to cut across the golf course.

Bonsai stood on the green of the first hole, next to the little flag. The tortoises can wait, I thought. Heartsong walked over to Bonsai.

As Heartsong approached the silver reindeer, however, I noticed that the yellow letters floating above Bonsai were different. I was still too far away to read them, but there were definitely more than six letters. The silver reindeer had changed his name, or else it was another reindeer entirely.

I kept walking until the letters became decipherable—the reindeer's name was LEAVETOWN.

As I approached, I could see that it was definitely Bonsai. At least the reindeer was identical: same size, colouring, hair. If so, why change his name? Was it a message to *me* to leave town?

Heartsong walked right up to the silver reindeer and stamped his right foot three times. No reaction. LEAVETOWN was sleeping.

I awoke to Patti standing beside my bed, shaking my legs. She had her green dress on again, her hair styled with a curling iron, her makeup done all professional. The bruise under her eye perfectly concealed. She looked amazing. I'd hire her on the spot if I was an IHOP manager.

"I'm off," she said. "You look hilarious in the morning. Wish me luck!"

It was nine-thirty—I'd slept through my alarm. So much for an early start.

Patti left for her interview, and I had a quick shower. The steam revealed a message written on the mirror: WINNER. I went down to Cinnabon, ate another cinnamon bun, and walked over to Fallsview. I wore one of Patti's scarves to hide the bottom half of my face, Patti's straw vacation hat, and my sunglasses. Patti's scarf smelled like bug spray, and I had to pull it down to my chin. No one would recognize me, hopefully. I was Annie Hart now.

I walked the floor of the casino, listening to the otherworldly chiming of the slot machines, searching for the Metro Man. I was leaning toward the theory that he'd never worked at Fallsview, that he was wearing the uniform for nefarious reasons. The bartender said he knew everyone and that he'd never seen that man in the vest before. The head of security claimed that the man had worked there, however, so I thought it wouldn't hurt to have another look. Maybe I'd see him. I wasn't holding my breath though. There was something a little off about the head of security.

I played a *Sex and the City* slot machine in case someone was watching me over the security cameras, wondering why the woman with her face all covered up was just walking around and not enjoying the games. I had a few good spins, lined up three Mr. Bigs at one point, and the five dollars I'd invested in the machines turned into thirty. I looked around to see if anyone noticed, if they were impressed. No one cared. I kept playing until the thirty disappeared, then resumed my search.

I was worried I'd see the man with the round glasses again, but he didn't show up. The bartender I'd talked to when I first came to the casino was working, so I stayed away from his bar. I was about ready to give up, considering my next move, when Patti called.

"They're giving me the job," she said, "but I have to work right now. They're short-staffed this morning and I have a chance to prove myself. The guy training me has a ridiculous voice and I'm trying not to laugh every time he says something. I'll be done around six. Don't leave, okay?"

"I'm supposed to have dinner with my mom. I was going to take a bus around four."

"Well, now you're not. Call her, she'll understand. We'll figure out a bus later. Just don't leave. We still need to check out that haunted house."

"I guess I could call her. Congratulations on the job. I guess you're really staying here?"

"Listen, I can't really talk right now. I just wanted to tell you I was working and to make sure you didn't leave. Anyway, don't go to Clifton Hill without me. We'll check out the haunted house together. It's too dangerous."

"Okay, but—"

"I said I can't talk now. Jesus, Colleen."

She hung up.

I walked the perimeter of the casino floor again, but the Metro Man wasn't there. Patti would get off work at six. It wasn't even eleven yet. So much time to fill. Time I couldn't waste. I left the casino, stepped outside. A dog was running around in the fountain. A man stood by the edge, clapping his hands, yelling, "Beanbag!" I called Mother. She didn't answer. That's okay, I thought. I wouldn't freak out. She was likely sleeping. I left her a voicemail, calmly asking her to call me back when she had a chance.

Several taxis were lined up along the street outside the casino. I looked at my phone. I wiped the smudges from my sunglasses with Patti's scarf. The man kept shouting, "Beanbag!" I walked up to one of the taxis and gave the driver a little wave. I got in.

"Clifton Hill, please," I said.

15

Clifton Hill was like a dream. My driver let me off next to a dinosaur-themed mini-golf course with life-size mechanical Tyrannosaurus rexes and velociraptors clawing at the air and a volcano looming over the play area. If I squinted, it looked like I really was in dinosaur times. I continued on. Children running around, licking huge swaths of neon cotton candy. A pair of identical twins wearing matching Planet Hollywood T-shirts. A Ferris wheel as tall as a hotel spun nearby. I walked up the street and saw novelty shops and rides everywhere. The sidewalks crowded with tourists. And there was the dumpster-sized Frankenstein's monster Patti had mentioned, eating a hamburger atop Burger King.

I passed several haunted houses, but all of them were open for business and none of them were called Mayhem Manor. I walked by a mirror maze, and then another mirror maze. A wax museum. Guinness World Records. Dairy Queen. Pizza Pizza. An arcade, a laser tag room, an enormous Boston Pizza. And then, after admiring the façade of a museum made to look like the Empire State Building had tipped over with King Kong hanging on the side, I turned down a small side street that drew fewer crowds. Sandwiched between two trinket shops stood Mayhem Manor.

Like Patti said, there was a notice posted on the door: TEM-
PORARILY CLOSED FOR RENOVATIONS. The glass door had been
covered up with brown paper on the other side, but there was a
small tear in the paper to the left of the notice. I cupped my hands
around my eyes and peered through the hole—too dark to see anything. I knocked and waited. Nothing happened. I turned around
and started walking away when I heard footsteps approaching
from inside. I stopped and looked back. The latch clicked. The
door popped open and a man leaned out. He was middle-aged, had
curly blond hair, and wore a Hawaiian shirt. I could see him being
handsome in a room filled with ugly men.

"Hi, there," the man said. "We're actually closed. Did you see
the sign?"

"Sorry, yes. I knocked and then saw it."

"There are other haunted houses in the neighbourhood. But
we'll be open in a few weeks, if you're still around."

"Okay, thanks." I turned back toward the more crowded street.

"Wait," the man in the Hawaiian shirt said. I turned around.
"You know what? If you want, I can let you through."

"That's okay."

"Seriously, we could use some feedback. Free entry, of course."

"No, but thank you. I was just curious."

"Come on, don't be shy. You'd be doing me a solid. We've completely changed the whole concept and I'd be interested to hear what
you think. It's not the final version, but you'll get the idea. It's mostly
the lobby that's under construction now. Trust me, you'll be nice and
scared. You're not pregnant, are you? Any heart conditions?"

The little voice in my head that sounded kind of like my mother
told me to walk away, that there was something sketchy about the
whole situation. The man with the round glasses had a key to this
place. He could be inside, waiting for me with a poison-filled
syringe. I was running out of time though. Maybe the key to the
whole Leonard affair could be found within Mayhem Manor.

"I'm not pregnant."

"That's the spirit." The man held the door open wide and stepped to the side. I went in.

Boxes were piled up on the counter next to the cash register. Wood stacked on the floor. Tools, extension cords, sawdust. No one else was around. The man in the Hawaiian shirt told me the rules—walk slowly, follow the red lights, yell "Let me out" if I got too scared—and then led me to a black curtain.

"I'll see you on the other side," he said.

I stepped through the curtain into complete darkness, aside from a red dot glowing in the distance. Like the little light on a smoke alarm or a VCR. Follow the red lights, the man had said. I walked into the blackness.

I braced for sudden noises, flashes of light, or mechanical dummy arms reaching out for my feet. But nothing happened. The wooden floor creaked, but otherwise the hallway was quiet. I walked slowly, my hands waving out in front of my body. When I got to the red light at the end of the hallway, I turned to see another red light on my left, down another dark hallway. I moved toward it.

Still, nothing was happening. No startling mechanisms, no ghostly recordings. Just darkness. Halfway down the hallway, I stopped. It felt like a lead sphere had dropped into my stomach. A terrible, queasy feeling low in my intestines. Nausea mixed with dread. At first, I thought that Mayhem Manor was simply doing its job—that the creators had succeeded in manufacturing a frightening experience. But that wasn't it. I leaned against the wall and began to count my breaths. A memory surfaced, from my adolescence. The Farm. The near pitch-black hallway I was traversing brought me back to Moon Camp.

When new recruits were brought to the Citizens of Light Rejuvenation Farm, they slept upstairs in Sun Camp. Sun Camp was a large room that took up half the upstairs, filled with bunk beds. Once Father Woodbine dreamt a recruit was ready to advance in their learning and responsibilities, he moved them down to Moon Camp in the basement. During the day, the door at the top of the basement stairs was left open and some light would make its way down. Sometimes Woodbine would descend with a flashlight or candle to make repairs or set up a bunk for a newly anointed Moon Camper. At night, however, the door was locked shut. The windows up by the ceiling, looking out onto the lawn, had all been boarded up. Lighters, matches, flashlights, electronic devices, and any other objects that emitted light were banned. From 9 PM to sun-up, we were left in the dark. Another attempt by Woodbine to simulate and normalize the death experience. He said that most people regularly communed with the Sun Spirit Ka without even realizing it, but they neglected the God-Spirit's other face. The dark face of the underworld and sacrifice. By spending these long hours living in the shadow of the Moon Spirit Ni, Woodbine said we would move closer to knowing the full God-Spirit Ka-Ni, until we reached a true enlightened state.

Standing there in the Mayhem Manor's hallway, a clear, specific memory of my time on The Farm came into focus. I was walking to the bathroom in the middle of the night. I had to pee and couldn't hold out until morning. It had been a few months already of living in Moon Camp and so I knew my way. A boy whose name I later learned was Lucas—we weren't allowed to use names on The Farm, since names were useless in death—was coughing in a nearby bunk. I could actually remember the sound of his cough echoing in that wet, cold basement that night. I continued on until I reached the bathroom, but the door was closed and locked. I tapped on the door lightly.

"Hello?"

No answer. I waited a minute and then tapped on the door again. I really had to go.

"Who's in there?"

Still no response. I waited a few more minutes, knocked a few more times, but all was quiet. The door at the top of the stairs was locked, so this was the only bathroom I could use. I jiggled the knob frantically, hoping that the door was just stuck, and then it happened. Warm liquid trickled down my legs and onto the floor. I walked back to my bunk, tucked my soiled underwear under the mattress, put on a fresh pair, and went to sleep. In the morning, I awoke to find out that one of the new Moon Campers, Christine, had sneaked rat poison from upstairs and swallowed it in the washroom after lights out. Woodbine had to break the door down. He found her lying on the floor, covered in vomit. She was only fifteen.

I hadn't thought of that in years, like it had been wiped from my memories. But it was back. I could smell Moon Camp. That damp, earthy smell returned to my brain as if I was lying in my bunk waiting for morning, when Father Woodbine would let us upstairs, and not stumbling around in a chintzy tourist attraction in Niagara Falls. I leaned my back against the wall. I was covered in sweat. What was I supposed to call out if I wanted to stop the experience? I couldn't remember the phrase.

"Stop!" I called out.

Nothing happened. I stood in the quiet, dark hallway.

"Hey!" I pounded on the wall with both fists. "I want out of here!"

16

A thud sounded from somewhere up ahead. I began to stomp across the floor, toward the red light, toward the sound. I flailed my arms in front of me. I screamed. I felt like when a bird gets trapped in a room full of people and starts flapping around. I reached the red light at the end of the hall and turned down the next one. Again, a red light in the distance. I continued to scream, to flail. And then, as I stomped forward, a beam of white came blinding into the darkness. I stopped, squinted. A door had opened. Light flooded the hall. There weren't any cotton cobwebs hanging from the ceiling, or any other thematic decorations or devices. It was just a hallway. Plywood floor, black walls. The man in the Hawaiian shirt stood in the doorway.

"Are you okay?" he asked.

"I need to get out," I said, hyperventilating.

"Of course. Right this way."

I followed the man through a closet-like room that led back into the lobby. I struggled to control my breathing.

"I'm so sorry," the man said. He walked behind the front counter and opened a door that led to a kind of office boardroom. There were two tables lined up end to end, a mini fridge, fluorescent lights on the ceiling. "I'll get you some water. Were you really that scared? Come sit down."

I sat at one of the tables. The man in the Hawaiian shirt filled a paper cup with water from a cooler and set it down in front of me. The AC made the room quite cold, but I was sweating. I downed the water in one gulp.

"They won't believe this," the man said. "I mean, I'm sorry you had a bad experience, but some of the other guys are skeptical about the new format. It was my whole idea, you know. Were you really that scared?"

"I'm sorry," I said. "I didn't mean to freak out like that."

"No need to apologize. It's supposed to freak you out. No, I'm sorry."

"I guess it wasn't what I expected."

"Right, yeah. I wanted to do something different from all the other haunted houses around here, you know? Make something that's actually scary."

"Maybe I don't understand," I said. "I mean, I did get scared. Clearly. But I think it was more that I was reminded of something from my past, which made me uncomfortable. Nothing actually happened in the haunted house. It was just the lights."

"Exactly. You didn't get the whole experience obviously, but that's pretty much the idea. It's what they call minimalism. We took out all the monsters and sound effects. We took out everything, actually. And when you get to the last hallway there's a way for us to loop you back to the beginning without you knowing. You end up in an endless circuit. It's more psychologically disturbing when you leave things to the imagination, right?"

"You're going to charge people to walk through dark hallways?"

"There's the red lights too. And your expectations are being played with because you know it's a funhouse. We're thinking of changing the name. Something with a little more class because the new haunted house is more intellectual. Minimalism, you know? 'Chateau de Mort' is one I came up with. Do you like that?"

"Sure."

"You do?" The man in the Hawaiian shirt stood up and clapped his hands. Started pacing. He poured himself a cup of water but just carried it around the room. "I can't wait to tell the guys. I need to get someone else in here to try."

I looked up at the clock—just after noon. I needed to get going. Then I noticed the large safe standing next to the water cooler. What is this place? I thought. I'd almost forgotten, in my panic, that the man in the round glasses had come here. A glass table covered with liquor bottles and tumblers sat in the corner of the room. What looked to be a cash counting machine rested on the table in front of me.

"What is this place?" I asked.

"I'm sorry?"

"This room. You have meetings in here?"

"Oh, no," the man said. He immediately stopped pacing and looked right at me. "This is just a room."

"What do you mean?"

"Nothing. It's just a room that we use to come up with ideas for the haunted house."

The man in the Hawaiian shirt had seemed relaxed and content, like a family dog. Now his brow was furrowed a little, his body tense. Like a dog without a family.

"I didn't mean to make you uncomfortable," I said. "I just thought it was interesting that there's this office inside a haunted house, that's all."

"I'm not uncomfortable."

"Good, no. I was just curious about it."

"I don't see why. Anyway, maybe I should get back to work."

"I'm sorry."

"Sorry for what? I'm not uncomfortable. I just realized the time, and I've got a lot to do. That's all."

"Okay."

I stood up. The man in the Hawaiian shirt stood by the door, staring down at the floor. On my way out of the room, I paused.

"Can I ask you something?"

"Sure," the man said. He attempted a smile, but I could tell he was frustrated with me now.

I pulled up the snapshot of the *Metro* photograph on my phone and handed it to him.

"You see that man in the background?"

I caught the surprise on his face when he saw the picture. His pupils dilated. Or shrank—something happened with his eyes. He composed himself quickly, but it was too late. He'd recognized the man in the vest.

"You *do* know him," I said.

"Sorry, no. Never seen him."

"You're lying."

"Honest, I don't. Who is he?"

"Please. I need your help. What about the name Leonard Weagle?"

"What the hell? Why are you really here? I thought you were just a tourist. Are you some kind of journalist?"

"Leonard was my husband. He's dead now. And he died under suspicious circumstances. Look." I retrieved my phone, opened up a photo of Leonard from his birthday. Captured a few months before his death. I took him and Mother to Denny's for a birthday breakfast and he wore his nice white shirt. My favourite picture of him. He'd gained these muscles from working extra hours at the plant, and he looked so strong. I remember having to practically beg him to get out of bed that morning, but we had a fun breakfast and he was glad he came. I passed it back to the man in the Hawaiian shirt. "That's Leonard."

"I'm sorry about your husband," he said. No surprised look this time—unless he'd simply gained control of his expressions. "But I've never seen him. What's going on? Who are you?"

"I'm trying to find the man from the first photo. He was at Leonard's funeral. I don't know his name. He lied to me about how he knew Leonard. I think he knows something about my husband's death. And when I asked about the man in the photo over at the casino, this creepy guy started following me around. The creepy guy came here afterward. He used a key to get in."

"I'm sorry, but—"

"Please!" I grabbed the man in the Hawaiian shirt's arm. He stepped back. "I don't want to cause trouble for you, but I need to know what happened to Leonard. I can't take it anymore. Did he owe you money? Or someone you work for? Was it gambling, or drugs? I'm begging you, please just tell me who this man is. I need to find him."

"You're here to find out what happened to your husband? That's what this is all about?"

"Please, help me. I need to know."

"I'm sorry. I wish I could help you out, really. I don't know what to tell you. I don't know this guy. And I've never heard of your husband."

"Please!"

"I'm sorry."

My senses were overloaded when I emerged from Mayhem Manor, back onto the streets of Clifton Hill. The overbearing sunlight, the tourists, the food smells. I pushed the heels of my hands into my eyes and leaned against an electric pole. Thirsty. My stomach was in knots—the stress of the last few hours, or maybe all the Cinnabon. And the heat. I couldn't possibly walk back to the hotel, which was where I definitely needed to go. I needed a bathroom, a bed. A few hours alone. I needed to call Mother.

I started walking toward the mini-golf course where the taxi had dropped me off in hopes of finding another ride, when someone tapped my shoulder. I shouted.

"Take it easy," a voice said.

I turned around. It was the man in the Hawaiian shirt.

"I just wanted to give you this," he said. He handed me a little flyer—it said Mayhem Manor in a blood splatter font. "I'm really sorry about your husband. I hope you can sort things out. Come back next month once we're up and running again. This is good for two people. Bring a friend. There's more info on the back."

"I don't want this," I said.

"Just hang on to it," he said, turning to leave. "You never know."

When I returned to our hotel room, I immediately called Mother, who, thank God, answered. She'd spent the morning reading *Under the Dome* and practising her harmonica.

"I play along with the TV," she said. "I put the music channel on and do backups. Don't ever tell anyone. Don't tell Patti. You're coming home tonight, right?"

"Of course," I said, though I wasn't sure. I mean, I had to go back. But there was still work to do in Niagara Falls. I just didn't know how to proceed.

"I'll take the lasagna out of the freezer and put it in the fridge to thaw. We can have a bit of apple crumble too. I saved some from last night. We can have a square each, or you can have two squares. I can't wait to see you, dear."

When we hung up, I washed my face, drank three mouthfuls of tap water, and climbed into my bed. I pulled the covers over my head and gripped the pillow tight. When I closed my eyes, I saw a red dot floating in the distance.

I awoke a few hours later, more tired than when I'd fallen asleep. I didn't want to get up, but I couldn't waste any more time. I had to do *something*. I checked my phone—just after four. I was supposed to meet Patti after work at six, then catch my bus home.

What could I possibly accomplish in that piddling amount of time? I could go back to Fallsview. I'd been all over that damn casino though. Regardless, my phone needed charging—I'd learned my lesson from the previous day. I plugged it in and pulled Leonard's laptop from my bag.

Bonsai was standing in the same spot as the day before, on the green of the first hole at Moroni Sands. The yellow letters floating above his head still read "LEAVETOWN." But now the golf course was filled with other reindeer.

There were about thirty of them. Heartsong stepped through the crowd. The new reindeer were identical: They all had the same appearance that you start the game with if you don't customize your character—medium height, brown fur, no markings. They were all asleep. And they all had the exact same name: 3408. The yellow number repeated itself across the golf course.

Thirty or so players, all inactive, all named 3408. The number seemed familiar, but I couldn't place it. The sight of all the sleeping reindeer was surreal. I was so used to the island being empty. It had to be some sort of server error. A game bug. Still, the whole thing felt unsettling. I shut the laptop. My phone had charged enough.

I decided to go to IHOP. I knew I should probably try the casino again, or do something productive, but I didn't want to be alone. I needed to think. And I was hungry. A pancake or two would be perfect, and maybe a milkshake if they had Mint Oreo or something in that flavour family. It was possible Patti would be my server. Hopefully she wouldn't be embarrassed. I wore my nice olive blazer, which Patti had complimented a few weeks earlier.

I walked along Fallsview Boulevard in the heat. I took off my blazer and you could see the sweat coming through my grey T-shirt. I crossed my arms. I passed by families and couples holding hands on the sidewalk. The only other person I saw walking alone was a teenage boy with a placard hanging from his neck that said PARKING $3.50/HR and had an arrow pointing up into the sky.

. I was steps away from Patti's IHOP when I heard a commotion behind me. I turned around. In the middle of the intersection I'd just crossed, a man on a bicycle was arguing with another man sitting on the ground.

"You're lucky I wasn't a car," the man with the bike said. "You can't just dart into the road like that."

"Oh, piss off," the man on the ground said. He stood up. He turned and looked directly at me.

It was Patti's husband.

He must have been following me. I turned back around. Kept moving.

"Colleen!" Dougie said. "Wait up!"

There was a lineup of families waiting in the IHOP entranceway. At the head of the line stood Patti, holding a stack of menus behind a little podium.

"Colleen?" Patti said. The people in line turned to look at me. The door slammed behind me.

"Dougie's coming. Right now. He saw me."

"And you came in here?"

"Oh, God. I'm so sorry."

"Okay, folks," Patti addressed the queue. "Someone will be right with you. Thank you for your patience. Colleen, come with me."

I moved to the head of the line and Patti grabbed my arm. The front door opened and Dougie walked in.

"Patti!" he said.

Patti and I ran down the hall, past the kitchen. She shoved me into the handicap washroom and followed me inside, locking the door.

"What the fuck were you thinking?" Patti whispered, her face panicked.

"I don't know. I was about to walk in when he saw me. I didn't know what else to do. Shit."

"It's my first day for Christ's sake."

We heard Dougie shouting things from the hallway.

"Patti," he said, his voice muffled, "we need to talk."

Then he started pounding on the washroom door.

"Let me in!"

Patti looked at me, holding her finger up to her lips. I placed my hand over my mouth.

"Come on, Patti," Dougie said. "I love you. We can work this out. I love you so much."

A woman joined Dougie outside the door. "Sir, I'm going to have to ask you to calm down."

"That's the manager," Patti whispered.

"I will not calm down," Dougie said. "That's my wife in there." He pounded on the door again.

"Excuse me, sir, but I'm afraid I'm going to have to ask you to leave."

"Patti!" Dougie said. "Let me in! I can make things right with you, Patti. I love you."

"Patti?" the manager said. "You in there?"

Patti sat down on the toilet. She was rubbing her hands on her thighs. Tears streamed down her face.

"Open the goddamn door!" Dougie said.

Things went on like this for another minute, until we heard another woman tell Dougie it was time to go. A walkie-talkie chirped static through the door—the woman was a security guard, or a police officer.

"You're in big goddamn trouble, Patti," Dougie said, before his voice disappeared down the hall.

The scene outside the door was quiet for a few minutes. Patti didn't say anything. Her face was buried in between her knees, her hands clasped around the back of her neck. I didn't say anything either. And then the doorknob jiggled.

"Patti," her manager said through the door.

Patti looked up at the door, then at me. I looked down at the floor.

"Patti," her manager said, again. "He's gone. It's safe now. You in there?"

"Yes," Patti said. "Colleen, open the door."

I opened the door.

Patti's manager, a short, froglike woman stood there with her hands on her hips. There were other people—men in aprons, a teenage girl holding a clipboard—standing behind the manager, peering into the washroom. Patti's manager stepped inside and closed the door.

The two women hugged. Patti explained her situation. The manager rubbed Patti's back. I leaned against the wall, stared at my hands. They didn't look real, somehow.

"Am I fired?" Patti asked.

"Hell no," the manager said. "I mean, you haven't actually been hired yet, so I can't really fire you anyway. But hell no, I'll keep you on. You came through today. With this situation you got going on here, it'd be nice if we can keep it away from the restaurant. You know, I had a situation just like this with an ex. Stress of it nearly destroyed my colon."

The manager continued to rub Patti's back. Patti's weeping continued, though it was less intense. She was calming down. I noticed something on the ground by Patti's feet—her hotel key card. I bent over and picked it up. I held it out to her, but she wasn't paying attention.

The key card was tucked into a little paper sleeve, with our room number written on the front in pen. I stared at the number until it began to blur.

3408.

18

Once we were assured that Dougie wasn't anywhere on the premises, Patti and I called a taxi and had it pull up around the back. We left through the kitchen and climbed into the cab. We kept our heads down as we drove back to the Queen Fallsview and scurried inside the hotel's front doors like celebrities during a scandal.

Patti and I both looked around nervously for Dougie as we waited for the elevator. Dougie was just one problem, however. Somebody out there knew our room number and knew they could find me in *Reindeer Island*. It didn't make any sense. I kept my eyes peeled for anyone that looked suspicious, which meant that everyone in the lobby looked suspicious, but nothing happened and we made it back to our room safely. No threats carved into our door. No manifestos scrawled on the bathroom wall with blood.

We sat down on our beds, and I gave Patti the rundown on all that had happened while she was serving customers at IHOP—my visit to Mayhem Manor, the red lights, the man in the Hawaiian shirt. The look on his face when I showed him the *Metro* photo. The strange office boardroom behind the counter, and the golf course populated with reindeer, all named after our hotel room number. Patti argued that the man from the haunted house was likely behind the *Reindeer Island* message. Or the man in the round glasses. Mayhem Manor, she figured, was used as a head-quarters for some criminal operation.

"The Russian scammers," Patti said. "It's connected to that somehow."

"But how did they find me in the video game?"

"They probably broke into our room last night while we were sleeping and hacked your computer."

"I don't know about that."

"I bet they have an inside guy who works here at the hotel, actually. He gave them our room key. They're probably watching us on a hidden camera right now."

"That's ridiculous. But we should probably move you to another hotel."

"Well, yeah. But we're already booked in here. No point in paying for two rooms. Just stay with me tonight and we'll keep each other safe. I'll change hotels tomorrow."

"I'm leaving, Patti."

"We'll see."

I decided to stay another night. It was getting late and Patti was frightened to be left alone, now that Dougie was running around the streets of Niagara Falls and some creep online knew our room number. Further, she argued, I was getting somewhere with my investigations. Stuff was happening, anyway. It would be a shame to abandon the mission now, with all the progress we'd made.

I called Mother to break the news—she answered on the first ring.

"Are you almost here, dear?" she said.

"I'm still in Niagara Falls. I'm staying another night. I'm sorry, Mother. Patti and I are having a really great time and it's just one more night."

"But the lasagna's in the oven. It's about ready."

"I'm sorry."

"Oh, don't be silly. I'm glad you're having a nice time with your friend. That's simply wonderful you're enjoying yourselves. I am a little worried about the lasagna though. Do you think it will reheat well?"

"Are you feeling okay? Will you be okay on your own for another evening?"

"Stay another week. Stay a month! I miss you, certainly, but that shouldn't stand in the way of your lovely vacation. The lasagna will have to be thrown out. It simply won't reheat well. I'll make a Costco run tomorrow morning and track down a new one."

"Patti and I are going out for dinner now," I said. "Call me if you need anything. Even if it's just that you can't find the remote, call me. I'll be home tomorrow for sure."

"You can stay in Niagara Falls for a year, if that's what you want. Though of course I'd be devastated."

We decided to eat at the restaurant on the top floor of our hotel. It seemed expensive, but we were hungry and it was close. We had to take the elevator up to the fortieth floor, and then get on a different elevator that took us up one floor to the restaurant. The elevator doors slid open and the hostess was standing right there smiling at us.

We sat down at a little table by the window, overlooking the boulevard, the casino, the falls. We ordered expensive glasses of white wine. An electronic candle flickered between us. Despite the classy ambiance, I couldn't relax. Whoever had left me the warning in *Reindeer Island* could be watching our table. I eyed the room suspiciously.

"What's the matter with you?" Patti said.

"Nothing," I said. "What should our next step be? We can't go back to Mayhem Manor. Can we?"

"Let's just have fun tonight. We haven't been able to enjoy our vacation together yet. We can start back up with the investigation or whatever tomorrow. Let's get drunk. We haven't been drunk together yet."

"I don't know."

"Trust me. Let's let loose for once. It's been a terrible fucking day. I want to have fun for five goddamn minutes."

We drank wine. I ordered this fancy pizza with goat cheese on it and Patti had ribs. A young man played covers on his acoustic guitar for the restaurant patrons. He wore a cute red bandana around his neck, like a Mimico dog coming back from the groomers. Patti got up to dance with some other young women when he played a Bruno Mars song. She pulled me out onto the dance floor but the song ended and I sat back down while the women were clapping.

"I'm gonna sleep with him," Patti said, rejoining me at our table. "I'm at least gonna make out with him. Did you see him eyeing me during the last song?"

"I think so," I said, though I didn't see anything like that.

"That little bandana's driving me nuts."

"So, it's really over with Dougie?"

"You're goddamn right it's over. You saw him today."

"What happened with him?"

"Nothing happened." Patti downed the last of her wine and sat up straight, scanning for our server. "Dougie's always been a prick. I guess I hit my limit. I'll be forty in a few years. I think I finally realized how I was squandering my time and attention on this awful person."

"I always thought you guys were happy."

"Nope."

"So, does he hit you? I mean you have that bruise . . ."

"Not anymore he doesn't."

"I'm so sorry, Patti. I didn't know."

"Why would you? Anyway, it's over. Fuck Dougie. I wasted an entire decade on that moron."

"How did you two end up together anyway?"

"I don't know. I honestly don't remember. I mean, I remember meeting him when we both worked at the mall, but I don't know why we started dating. I guess he was more attractive back then. Less angry, or at least he didn't show it so much around me. And then I thought I was pregnant and he proposed. Later I found out that it was just bird flu, but we got married anyway."

"You thought you were pregnant because you had the flu?"

"Bird flu. Jesus Christ, Colleen. This is depressing. I thought we were supposed to be letting loose."

"I know. I'm sorry."

"No, it's okay. I shouldn't be complaining, what with the hell you're going through. I can't believe you're a widow."

"It's okay."

"You know what, Colleen?" Patti said, leaning over the table toward me. The flicker of the electronic candle gave her face this important aura, like she knew important secrets about the universe. "I'm glad you're here with me. I wish you would stay in Niagara Falls."

"I wish I could too."

"I mean, you can."

"I know."

"But your mother."

"But my mother."

"Well, I'm glad you're here now."

The waiter refilled our glasses. I started feeling tipsy. The room seemed friendlier. Patti and I were laughing. She was staring at the guitarist in the bandana and telling me all the dirty things she wanted to do to him. I got the giggles. I forgot about Leonard and my grief. I was present in the moment, there with Patti at our table overlooking the lights along the boulevard. We finished our wine and the waiter brought us each another glass. We toasted

Niagara Falls.

"I'm gonna go talk to him," Patti said. The young man in the bandana had finished his set and was packing up his acoustic guitar. "Mama's getting a phone number."

On her way over, however, a group of college girls surrounded the musician and Patti came back to the table.

"I guess *that*'s why I stayed with Dougie so long," Patti said.

"What do you mean?"

"I don't know. Let's go back to the room."

Patti turned out the lights, put on the TV, and got into bed. Another episode of *Dateline*—a woman shot her mail carrier and later claimed she'd thought he was a ghost. Patti fell asleep and I took my screenplay notebook into the washroom.

I sat up against the wall with the notebook open in my lap, but I didn't write anything. I didn't think anything, either. I stared at the towel hanging from the rack opposite from me. The room felt a little like it was spinning. Something crinkled in my back pocket. I pulled it out—the flyer the man in the Hawaiian shirt had given me. I unfolded the paper and laughed. There was a cartoon of a man with a bloody axe. Part of his brain was showing. Mayhem Manor didn't have anything like that. They didn't have anything at all. I turned the flyer over.

There was something written on the back, in pen: ROS-WELL'S 6 PM.

19

I awoke at seven with a headache. My stomach was in turmoil. I drank some water from the bathroom sink and then had a painful bowel movement. Patti was still sleeping when I came out of the washroom. I wanted to tell her about the message I'd found on the back of the flyer. I wasn't sure if the note was meant for me or not, but I'd Googled "Roswell's Niagara Falls" and discovered it was a restaurant in town. If I stuck around until the evening, I could stop by the restaurant at six. See who showed up. I needed Patti's advice. I didn't feel right about waking her, though, so I went down to the lobby to buy us each a Cinnabon. While I was waiting in line to order, I noticed a glowing red dot on the ceiling. Security camera. I remembered following the red dots in Mayhem Manor. I remembered remembering the darkness of the basement on The Farm, waiting for the bathroom. For a split second, I was back there. I was standing outside the bathroom door in Moon Camp, knocking quietly. A sweet young girl named Christine lay dead on the other side.

"No," I said, there in the Cinnabon queue. The man in front of me turned and looked at me. I also turned and looked around, but there wasn't anyone behind me.

Sometimes I'd remember little things from Father Woodbine's cult. An image or scene would flash across the projection screen in my head. Usually at night, while lying in bed. I'd try and block it out and think of something more pleasant. Remembering life with the Citizens of Light always made me feel uneasy, nauseous, or like menacing things were waiting around every corner. I talked about my cult days with the psychologist I had to see after I was released, but once those sessions ended, I had no reason to bring it up. Mother never pressed me. She knew what I went through.

Once, I unloaded a hefty pile of Woodbine memories onto Leonard. This was a year or so into our marriage. I came home from work one evening to find Leonard asleep in our bed. He had a library copy of *My Year in the Shadows* under his arm. This was the book Lacy had written. I would skip to another shelf if I came across it in a bookstore. There were likely photos of me in there, but I refused to crack the spine.

"Leonard." I shook him awake. "What the hell is this?"

I threw the book at the wall.

Leonard apologized. He squeezed my hands and begged for forgiveness. He said he just wanted to know my whole story. Like he was missing out on a significant part of what made me who I am. I screamed and stomped out of the room. I walked around the block twice before I began to calm down. I sat down on our front steps, caught my breath. He was right, I realized then. He was my husband. He deserved to know the story.

The next evening, Leonard and I were eating A&W burgers in the Sherway Gardens food court. We'd been filing our taxes at the H&R Block. We weren't really talking. I started telling him about the cult.

I gave him the basics—how I was recruited at the bus station, the Moon Camp in the basement, the beheading videos. How we grew most of our own food, along with marijuana, and sold both our legal and illegal crops to help fund the operation. I spoke carefully, calmly. When I finished, I started to cry.

"It's okay," Leonard said, handing me a napkin from the stack on his tray. "I know how hard it is for you to talk about this stuff. But it's important for you to let it out. Keep going. What was Father Woodbine really like? Do you remember any of his teachings?"

Just then, the old man sitting at the adjacent table leaned over and asked if we'd watch his stuff while he went to the bathroom. A plastic No Frills bag lay on his table. Leonard gave him a thumbs up and then looked at me.

I started crying again. Louder this time. Leonard gripped my shoulders and looked into my eyes.

"Hey," he said. "You're doing great. Don't stop now."

"Not now," I said, blowing my nose into a napkin.

"Please. Colleen, you can do this. Start with Woodbine. What was he like?"

I did my best to answer Leonard's questions, but the crying just got worse. People were staring. I tried to whisper my recollections but then Leonard couldn't hear me and he made me repeat myself. I hated Leonard in that moment. His expression seemed too eager, like he was enjoying hearing about the cult. A sadistic shadow on his brow. Of course, he only wanted to get closer to me. I'd been hiding a significant part of my life from him, and he wanted to share my burden. I gave him all the information I could manage until I began to shake, and then Leonard relented. He placed his hands on my knees under the table.

"Stop," he said. He'd been crying too. "I'm sorry. I shouldn't have pressed you. I don't know what's wrong with me. I'm so sorry, Colleen."

I wanted to leave, but we couldn't. We were in charge of the old man's bag. It lay flat, like there was a magazine or a calendar inside. Fifteen minutes had already passed since the man left. The washrooms were within my line of sight. I stared at the entrance, praying for the old man to appear, but he'd vanished. Eventually Leonard went to check if he was okay, but he wasn't in the bathroom. We opened the No Frills bag. Inside were loose papers covered in crude pornographic drawings. Men with enormous penises groping enormous, disembodied breasts. We placed them back in the bag and left. Leonard and I never spoke of my time in the cult again.

Patti was awake when I returned to our room. I filled her in on the message about Roswell's.

"This is crazy," Patti said. "I mean, it's probably nothing. But we have to go. What's the menu like?"

"We're not going to actually eat. I just need to see who shows up. Maybe the man from the haunted house has information for me."

"What if it's a date?"

"What do you mean?"

"He gave you a note with the name of a fancy restaurant and the time written on it. Sounds like a date to me."

"I don't know that it's fancy. It's not a date."

"What did he say when he handed it to you? Is he hot?"

"He just said to come back next month when the haunted house is finished. But he did say there was more info on the back of the flyer."

"He did? Well, there you go."

"I don't know. It could be nothing, but it also could be that this man is trying to help us. I told him about Leonard and he did seem a little concerned. At least he acted that way. It's definitely not a date."

"Well, we can't show up and peep through the window. We need to sit down and order."

"What if it's a trap? I guess that sounds crazy. But the guy who followed me at the casino could be waiting there for us."

"So what? What's he going to do? Actually though, I'm wondering if we should go in disguise. That way we can arrive early, grab a table in the corner. If someone does show up, we can see what they do. Like in a spy movie. Like in *Austin Powers*. And it's probably nothing anyway. We'll have a nice meal."

"I don't know."

"Well, I'm curious now. I'm going no matter what."

"You can't go there alone, Patti."

"Then it's settled."

I packed my bag and then I helped Patti pack her bags. We went down to the lobby and waited in line to check out. We both wore scarves, sunglasses, layers. Patti decided to return to the Captain's Inn. It was cheap, it was familiar, and it wasn't too far from the IHOP. After our room number was plastered across the screen in *Reindeer Island*, she couldn't possibly stay on at the Queen Fallsview by herself. I tried not to react when the man at the counter handed me our bill, but the number written at the bottom was insane and I winced. I paid with Mother's credit card. We took the elevator down to the underground parking and drove out to a paid lot closer to the Captain's Inn. Patti parked in the back, between two trailers. One of the trailers had a bumper sticker on it that said HONK IF YOU LOVE THE RAT PACK. We walked the ten minutes to Patti's new lodgings, the sun rising overhead, the temperature climbing. It was hot, but not sweltering yet.

Patti spotted a dead raccoon floating in the Captain's Inn pool. She told the kid at the reception desk about it when we walked into the office. The kid wrote POOL on a scrap of paper and tucked it in his breast pocket.

We brought our bags up to her room, which stood across the hall from our old one. The same ugly brown carpet, with similar stains. That stale, acrid smell. A single bed this time.

"This will have to do for now," Patti said. She sat down on the edge of the bed and turned on the TV. "Lance from work said he might know of a room in town. Most of the others live in St. Catharines, but I want to be here. Close to the action, you know?"

"I can't believe you live in Niagara Falls," I said, sitting at the desk next to the TV stand. "Work won't be the same. If I even work there anymore. I missed yesterday's shift and I'm going to miss tonight's."

"That's why you should move here. I'm just saying."

"I know. Anyway, what's the plan? Are we really going to Roswell's?"

"We need disguises. There's got to be a costume place around here. Let's look it up."

The Wi-Fi wasn't working, so we went down to ask the kid at reception about costume stores in town.

"What kind of costumes?" the kid said.

"Does that matter?" Patti said.

"I guess not. Anyway, I don't know of any stores like that."

"Thanks anyway," I said. We turned to leave.

"Wait," the kid said. "Stay out of the pool. Apparently, there's a raccoon in there."

We walked back to Patti's car and drove around, looking for a costume store. We found a second-hand clothing place near Clifton Hill. I picked out a pair of baggy jeans, an oversized flannel shirt, and a yellow trucker hat with a picture of a rifle scope on it. With my sunglasses, I wouldn't be instantly recognizable, at least. It would have to do. Patti went with men's grey jogging sweats and a black toque, like Rocky in training. She said she'd give herself stubble with mascara. We were ready.

"What's our backstory?" I asked. "I'll be Annie Hart. But what are we doing in Niagara Falls? Maybe we're sisters on a road trip to the east coast."

"Our backstory is that it's nobody's business."

"But shouldn't we be prepared in case someone asks?"

"If someone asks, you tell them it's none of their business."

Back at the Captain's Inn, I called Mother. I wouldn't be making it home for dinner. Depending on how things went at the restaurant, it could be a late night. I needed to see things through. Mother said she didn't mind, but I could hear the quiver in her voice. I felt terrible. Stringing her along, lying to her about my true purpose in Niagara Falls.

"I'm so sorry," I said. "I'll try not to be too late."

"Don't be sorry," Mother said. "I'm absolutely fine. I'm over the moon about you having such a nice trip. If you say you're sorry one more time, I'm hanging up the phone. Of course, I would never, but you get my meaning."

"But I am sorry."

"I forbid it!"

We arrived at Roswell's at 5:45. The restaurant was flying-saucer themed. The servers wore emerald-green uniforms. There were framed newspaper clippings about UFO sightings and alien abduction scares on the walls. A giant *X-Files* poster. Chubby Checker playing, or someone similar. I'm not sure how that tied into the theme. The dining room was mostly empty. No sign of the man in the Hawaiian shirt, yet. We sat at a table in the corner opposite the entrance. I sat with my back to the door, but Patti was able to see who entered the restaurant.

"Do I want the Out of this World burger?" Patti said, her face buried in the menu. "Or the Mars cheeseburger? I've been eating a lot of burgers lately."

"Maybe you should keep an eye on the door. I can read the menu to you."

"And there's the Beam Me Up bacon burger. Their fries are called Alien fries. That seems lazy."

"Patti? Why don't you let me read the menu to you? I'm worried someone will come in and you won't see."

"It's fine, I'm glancing up and checking. Look, there's an Out of this World salad. They reused that one."

"This was a bad idea. What if it's a trap?"

"It's *fine*. Jesus Christ. What are you gonna get?"

"You're not looking up. You haven't looked up once since you said that's what you were doing."

"Here," Patti said, making a real show of looking around the room, her neck protruding and eyes bulging. "Okay?"

"Maybe we should switch seats. But no, I can't do that. Let's just leave."

"Will you calm down? Nobody is going to recognize you. We're fine."

"Can I at least read you the menu? It's making me—"

"Oh my God."

"What?"

"He's here. He just walked in."

"What?" I whispered. Leaned over the table, closer to Patti. "How do you know? Is he wearing a Hawaiian shirt?"

"No, it's *him*."

"Who?"

"The man from Leonard's funeral."

20

When Patti assured me that it was safe to look over, I turned around. It really was him. The wide face and beady little eyes were unmistakable. The Metro Man, in the flesh. He wore a dress shirt and tie, his blond hair slicked back. Talking to a server. I spun back around to face Patti.

"My God." I leaned over the table and whispered. "What do we do?"

"You can talk normally. He's on the other side of the frigging room."

"Do you think he's waiting for someone else?" I said, a touch louder. "The guy from Clifton Hill?"

Just then a man in an emerald-green polo appeared, crouching down at our table.

"Evening, folks," he said. Big smile. "I'll be taking care of you fine people today. I'm Bradley." He took a marker out of his breast pocket and scrawled the word Bradley onto the paper tablecloth.

"Hi, Bradley," Patti said.

"I'll bring you each a glass of Niagara's finest," Bradley said, standing up. "Are we doing ice? No ice? I have sparkling water too. What are we thinking?"

"Tap is fine," Patti said. "Yes, ice."

"Decisive, I love it!" Bradley said. "And have you had a chance to look at the drink menu yet? I feel like I'm getting a margarita vibe from you two. What's the plan here?"

"Water's fine," Patti said.

"Just water for now, thank you," I said.

"Keeping it simple, I love it!" Bradley said.

Patti and I both ordered the Mars cheeseburger and split a plate of Alien fries. I couldn't eat though. Not with that man in the same room. I couldn't decide if I should walk over and confront him or keep my distance and watch what he did. Follow him out of the restaurant. If I went up to him and things didn't go well, that would be it. I'd have blown my chance. I wasn't even sure what to say. I needed more information. Maybe find out his name, where he lived. But if I did try and follow him, I could screw that up too. We might lose him. Another chance blown.

"We won't lose track of him," Patti said. "People say I'm an incredible driver. I can keep up with that asshole."

"It's not just that. He's right here. This could be my best shot."

"Then go over there."

"I can't."

"Why not?"

"Let's just see what he does. What's he doing now?"

"I was going to say, he's been staring at this one waitress. It's a bit weird. You can look."

I turned around. The Metro Man had his hands clasped together on the table and he was kind of leaning forward, turning his head to face the corner of the room opposite us. It looked like he was watching one of the servers, who was cleaning glasses behind the bar.

"Maybe he's been waiting a while for her to take his order?" I said, turning back to Patti.

"Nah, she's not his server. He's got Bradley."

"My ears are burning," Bradley said in a sing-song voice, sidling up and crouching at our table again. "Just wanted to check in and see how we're finding those first few bites. Are we loving the burgers? Are we in heaven right now?"

"It's fine," Patti said.

"What about you?" Bradley said, looking at me. "Are we in hamburger heaven?"

"That man sitting by himself near the bar," I said. "Wearing a tie. Are you waiting on him?"

"I am, yes," Bradley said. "Why do you ask?"

"Do you know him?"

"Isaac? Yes, of course. Comes in every night."

"Really?"

"Sure, yeah. I've only been working here a few months, but apparently Isaac's been coming in for years. Six o'clock on the dot, every evening."

"So, he must live nearby?"

"I believe he's in the neighbourhood, yes. Do you know him?"

"Just curious."

"Curiosity, amazing!" Bradley slapped his hands together and stood up. "Alright, what can I get you ladies? Side of mayo? Perhaps you're ready to hop aboard the margarita train?"

"Bring us the bill, please," I said.

"Colleen," Patti said, "I'm not—"

"Trust me," I said. "Bill please, Bradley."

I paid up, leaving Bradley a generous tip. We snuck past the Metro Man—or Isaac, apparently—and out into the parking lot. He didn't look at us. We got into Patti's car, and I had her drive over to the back corner of the lot, where we had a clear view of everything. Now that I knew his name and that he lived nearby, it seemed like a good idea to gather more information before confronting him. By paying up early, we could be sure to watch Isaac leave the restaurant and follow him home. Or wherever he went. Maybe he'd lead us somewhere incriminating and we could call the police.

"Which car do you think is his?" Patti said.

"I don't know," I said. "Could be any of these. Or he could be on foot, if he lives nearby."

"Shit, how do we follow him if he's walking? Drive all slow, like some pedophile in a van?"

"I guess we could walk. I feel safer in the car though. Maybe he drove here."

"I need to run in and use the washroom real quick."

"Patti, you can't. He could leave."

"I'll be like lightning," Patti said, opening her door. "Anyway, there's nothing I can do about it. Be right back."

"Please, just try and hold it."

"You can't hold diarrhea, Colleen."

I stared at the entrance to Roswell's, willing Patti to emerge. What was taking her so long? I dug my fists into my thighs. Drummed my feet on the floor. Eventually, someone did walk out of the doors I'd been fixated on. It wasn't Patti. It was Isaac.

"Oh," I said.

Isaac walked over to the sidewalk and headed east, away from me. He left my view as he passed in front of the restaurant. I no longer had eyes on him. No sign of Patti. He could be getting into a car. Or walking down a side street. Entering a shop.

"Oh no," I said.

I shuffled over into the driver's seat. The keys were still in the ignition.

As I turned out of the lot onto the street, I could see Isaac walking up ahead. About a block away. I needed to maintain that distance between us. I drove ahead a little, then pulled over to the curb. If I shuffled along like this, I thought, driving forward and pulling over in fits and starts, I would draw suspicion. And, like Patti had pointed out, I'd creep him out if I drove along too slowly. Like the classic pervert in a van. Following him on foot was out of the question—I felt too vulnerable. I needed Patti. I spun around to see if she was out in the parking lot yet, looking for her car. She wasn't.

I drove forward, slowly. Isaac continued east on the sidewalk. Strolling casually, it seemed. Like he didn't have a care in the world. Nothing on his conscience. Probably whistling. I should just run him down and be done with it, I thought.

Isaac left the commercial strip, walking into a residential area. Less traffic, less people. Easier to spot him from a distance, and easier for him to spot me. I pulled over and waited a minute for the gap between us to widen before I made the turn.

We were in a relatively affluent neighbourhood. Two-storey houses, nice cars in the driveways. Plenty of trees. Well-maintained lawns. Isaac was still a block away from me. He made a right down another street. I pulled over again and waited thirty seconds before following him.

When I turned onto this new street, I was shocked to find Isaac standing still on the sidewalk, about ten feet from me. Instinctively, I hit the brakes. Isaac, who had been staring down at his phone, looked up at me. I immediately ducked down, then realized how suspicious that would be. I shot back up. I adjusted the rear-view mirror, using my arm to block my face, then started driving forward. Isaac returned to his phone—he hadn't recognized me, it seemed. I drove past him.

What now, I thought. I could pull over up ahead and watch him in the mirrors. See if he turned down another street. If he didn't turn, however, he'd walk right past me. I'd already had one close call. I needed Patti. Maybe she could taxi over and follow him from behind, somehow. We could coordinate together. I drove ahead and went down the next side street. Pulled over. I took out my phone and called Patti. I felt her phone vibrate under my leg.

I stepped out of the car and jogged back to the intersection. I crept up behind a large bush planted in the corner of someone's lawn and peered out, back down the road where I'd last seen Isaac. I could see a figure in the near distance, walking toward me. Too dark to make out their features, but it had to be him. I was about to run back to the car when the figure crossed to the other side of the road. It was definitely Isaac. He was talking on the phone. And then he walked up a driveway. One of the smaller houses. One-storey, no garage. A grey Camry parked outside. I took my phone from my pocket and snapped a picture of the house.

"Hey, you!" a voice called out.

I turned around.

A man in a gold-coloured bathrobe stood in the doorway of the house behind me. I was crouched behind his bush.

"What are you doing sneaking around on my property?" the man said.

I didn't say anything. I looked over at the small house across the road—Isaac had disappeared inside, apparently.

"Hey!" the man said.

"I was trying to get a picture," I said. "There was a deer."

"A deer? In this neighbourhood?"

"I almost had the shot, too. Then *you* came and scared it off."

"I didn't realize," the man said. "I'm so sorry, miss."

Before returning to the car, I walked closer to the house Isaac had entered and took a picture. I made note of the address: 310 Maldon Road. Then I drove back to Roswell's.

Patti was talking to someone when I pulled into the lot. Green uniform. The server that Isaac had been staring at. She went back inside the restaurant and Patti ran over. A cigarette in her hand. I stepped out of the car.

"What happened?" Patti said, out of breath. "Did you follow him?"

"I think I found his place. We should head back over there. We'll stake it out. Are you smoking?"

"Gathering intel." Patti threw the cigarette on the ground.

Patti told me that when she'd left the washroom, she noticed that Isaac's table was empty. She ran out into the parking lot, saw that me and the car were gone, and figured out what had happened. While she was waiting for me to return, the server Isaac had been watching came outside for a smoke break. Patti thought she might know something about Isaac, since he apparently came in every night. She asked the server, whose name was Jess, for a cigarette. They started talking. Patti asked Jess about the strange man who'd been staring at her while she cleaned the glassware.

"His full name's Isaac Kindler," Patti said. "He and Jess used to date actually, briefly, years ago. A real oddball, she says. Harmless but strange. He's obsessed with her. Comes in for dinner every night, in case she's working. Just so he can be around her. She feels bad for him, because I guess he's kind of a lonely guy—doesn't have much going on. She says she tries not to encourage him and won't wait on his table, but she puts up with him coming in all the time. I know *I* wouldn't let some creep stalk me like that."

"Oh my God. Did she say if he works at the casino?"

"I asked. She doesn't know. She said she doesn't think he does anything, really. I guess his family has money and he just loafs around, or that's her impression. This is fucked. What's his place like?"

"You'll see in a minute. Let's go."

We parked on Maldon Road, a few houses down from the place Isaac had entered. The lights were still on, the curtains closed. Patti and I sat in the dark. If anyone walked up to the car and peered in, they'd probably see us, but Isaac wouldn't if he looked out at the street from his window. And there was no one else around. Zero traffic. A quiet, suburban neighbourhood, five minutes from the chaos of Clifton Hill.

"Are we going to stare at his house all night?" Patti said.

"Let's just wait a little while. Maybe he'll come out. And when those lights go off, I'm going to go snoop around."

"What are you going to find? A patch of lawn he forgot to mow?"

"Maybe there'll be some mail. Maybe there's a shed back there that I can get into. I don't know, we'll see."

"That seems a bit dangerous. We don't know who this guy is."

"Exactly. Let's find out."

"What if we came back tomorrow night? If he goes to Roswell's every night at six, he'll go tomorrow."

"If this is actually his house. And if he lives alone."

"It has to be his place. Bradley said he lived around here. And Jess said he's this lonely guy. There's no one else in there. Maybe a sex doll with Jess's photo taped over the face."

"We could come back, I guess. But then I'd have to stay another night."

"Oh please. It's like eight-thirty now. You're driving back to Toronto?"

"Well, I was supposed to. My mother's waiting for me."

"Jesus Christ, Colleen. You're staying another night."

"I am?"

"You are."

I stepped out of the car so I could call Mother in private. I felt terrible for leaving her alone again. I kept dashing her hopes at the last second, too. Torturing her. But there was nothing I could do—I had to stay. I leaned against the trunk and pulled my rifle scope hat down over my eyes. After two rings, I heard a door shut behind me. I turned around—it was Isaac. I hung up my phone and ducked down behind the car. Isaac locked his front door and walked into the driveway. He didn't look over. He got into his Camry and backed out onto the street. I crawled behind the driver's side of Patti's car as he passed by.

"Holy shit," Patti said, opening her door. "Should we follow him?"

"I don't know."

"Well, there's no time to think. We have to go now."

"Well then forget it. Let's go check out the house."

Patti said something else, but I was already halfway across the lawn.

I knocked on the front door, just to be sure. Also, it made things a touch less suspicious if a neighbour was watching. Just an old friend, stopping by. No one answered. I got down on my knees and opened the mail slot—a touch more suspicious—but I couldn't see anything.

Patti walked up to the porch, clutching the ice scraper from her car.

"What's that for?"

"It's a weapon. I don't know."

"Let's look around back."

I led her across the driveway and around the side of the house. I didn't hear any dogs barking, which was good. We passed by a trash bin—if there were bags in there, we could go through them for evidence. After we checked out the yard. I kept moving.

The backyard was small, about the size of my kitchen. Isaac shared a fence with the neighbours on all three sides, but there wasn't anyone outside and the shrubbery obscured things anyway. No shed to investigate. Just some boards piled up under a tarp, a snow shovel leaning up against the fence. The sliding door leading out into the backyard was locked. The curtains were drawn so I couldn't see anything. And then I noticed the air conditioner. Sticking out of the window a few feet from the sliding door, sitting at about shoulder-height. It wasn't running. I reached up and pushed. It wouldn't budge, like it was screwed to the window. I needed more leverage.

"What are you frigging doing?" Patti whispered.

I took the snow shovel from the fence and brought it over to the window.

"Colleen!" Patti said. "What the fuck? The neighbours."

I wedged the shovel underneath the AC unit and shoved. I had to use all my strength, but eventually there was a cracking sound. I kept pushing. Another big crack, and then a thud as the air conditioner hit the floor, inside the house. I set down the shovel.

"What did you do?" Patti said.

"Quiet," I said.

We listened. No alarm. No dogs. The neighbours didn't seem to have noticed.

"Alright," I said. "Boost me up."

22

The house was dark. I turned on my phone's flashlight and scanned the room. I stood in Isaac's kitchen. The air conditioner and some splintered wood from the window lay at my feet in a small puddle of water. The house was quiet. I nudged the air conditioner out of the way with my foot and stuck my head back out the window.

"I'll unlock the door," I said.

"This has gone too far," Patti said. "We need to leave."

I shut the window, walked into the dining room, and opened the sliding door. Patti stood outside, motionless.

"Come on," I said.

"You come on," Patti said. "This is ridiculous. I'm out of here."

I turned back into the house. Patti followed me inside and shut the door. I scanned the area with my phone's flashlight. Isaac's place was clean, tidy. A framed poster of the Three Stooges on one wall. A framed poster of an old-timey guy playing pool on another. Nothing on the dining room table but a laptop. I opened it up and a password prompt appeared on the screen. Maybe I'd find the password written down somewhere, I thought. I moved into the living room, Patti following right behind me. A couch, an empty coffee table, a bookcase. A framed photograph of Elvis Presley holding a pistol. A large TV. Several small succulents on the TV stand. And then I saw it: on Isaac's bookcase, a copy of *My Year in the Shadows*.

"Oh my God," I said.

"What?"

"Nothing. Sorry, thought I saw something."

I pulled the book from the shelf. I opened it to where a bookmark had been placed, about halfway through. Text on the left page and a photo of Father Woodbine on the right. Sitting in court, smiling. Those curly tufts of hair blooming around his ears. Those buck teeth, those wild eyes. I hadn't seen a picture of him in a decade, at least. When I was sixteen, I'd thought he was so handsome and charming. Now he just looked silly. Like a happy hobo in an old cartoon.

"Who is that?" Patti said, looking over my shoulder.

"I don't know," I said. I placed the book back on the shelf.

Patti didn't know that I'd been part of a cult as a teenager, and this wasn't the right moment to bring her up to speed. But it was interesting that Isaac had *that* book in his home. Although, it had been a bestseller, plenty of people had copies of *My Year in the Shadows*.

There was an office and a bedroom down the hall. I checked the office first, Patti following behind me. Another computer—it also required a password to log on. Some more books. Mostly stuff about old Hollywood and vaudeville. A collection of Peanuts strips. An Elvis biography. A lot of conspiracy books: the Illuminati, lizard people, mind control. I went through the desk. There were some papers in one of the drawers, but nothing interesting. Banking and tax stuff. A doodle of a toilet. Nothing to do with Fallsview Casino. His name was indeed Isaac Kindler. The other desk drawers were locked.

"Look for a key for these," I said. "Or we could just break them open."

"This is a bad idea, Colleen. What if he comes back? We need to leave."

"See what's in this closet. I'm gonna check the bedroom."

Isaac's twin bed was immaculately made, like in a hotel. There was an amateurish painting on the wall of a barn burning down at night. An odd thing to put up in your bedroom, I thought. That day's *Niagara Advance* on the bedside table. A closet full of pants and shirts and suit jackets that looked dull and pricey. I went back to the office. Patti was hunched over, digging through a box in the closet.

"You find anything?" I asked.

"Bunch of photographs. Mostly old vacation and family stuff. I found a few of Isaac and Jess the server. But then there's these weird ones of someone's house at night, shot from across the street. This guy coming in and out of the house. They look like surveillance photos. Take a look."

"Why would he have these?"

"I don't know. Did you find anything?"

The room suddenly became illuminated. The hallway light had been turned on.

I froze. Patti froze too, a look of terror on her face. Then the sound of creaking wood. Light footsteps approaching from the hall. I turned around. A figure appeared in the doorway. It flicked on the office light. It was Isaac. Clutching a golf club.

I screamed.

"What the hell?" Isaac said. "My God, Colleen?"

Isaac stared at me from the doorway. A look of confusion on his face. Patti had scooted back into the corner and was sitting against the wall. Clutching her ice scraper. I backed up so that I was standing beside her.

"Are you going to tell me what the heck is going on here?" Isaac said.

"I'm sorry," I said.

"Who is this?" he said, gesturing toward Patti. I'd forgotten how reedy his voice was—it had surprised me when I met him at the funeral. He sounded like a comedian doing a scientist character. "What are you two doing here? How did you get in?"

"The window. I knocked your air conditioning unit inside."

"Why?"

"Are you going to hurt us?"

"What?" Isaac looked at the golf club in his hands and set it down on the floor. "Of course not. But you might want to tell me what you're doing in my house."

I looked down at the floor. I opened my mouth to speak, but hesitated.

"Colleen," Isaac said.

"Something happened to my husband."

"Okay—"

"There's more to the story. I know there is. He was mixed up in something before he died. And you lied to me. At Leonard's funeral. You said you worked at the plant with him, and I know that you didn't."

"Oh, geez," Isaac said. He leaned back against the doorframe and rubbed his eyes with his fingertips. "That's what this is? Because of what I said to you at the funeral?"

"Yes!" I was shaking. "I need to know the truth."

"We were in the program together."

"The program?"

"AA. I was Leonard's sponsor. This was years ago, when I lived in Toronto. But yeah. You're not supposed to break the anonymity of members. When you asked, I said we worked together."

"But I'm his wife. Leonard's dead. Why couldn't you just have told me the truth?"

"You're not supposed to break the anonymity of members. It doesn't matter if they're family, or if they've passed on. That's the whole darn idea."

"Right. Yeah, I guess so."

"Anyway, I sure am sorry. I didn't realize what an effect this lie would have on you. If I had known, I would've just told you the truth."

"Hold on," Patti said, pushing herself up off the ground. She stood up next to me. Pointed the ice scraper at Isaac. "It's more than that. There was a guy at the casino who followed Colleen after she asked about you. And then the guy at the haunted house told us where to find you. Who are all these shady people that seem to be in your orbit?"

"What the heck are you talking about?" Isaac said. "What guy at the casino? What haunted house? Who *are* you?"

"She's with me," I said. "And she's right. We've definitely encountered a lot of suspicious people since we started looking into you."

"Go break into *their* homes then. How did you even find me?"

"I saw a photo of you in the paper. Working at the casino. That's how I knew where to look for you."

"What paper?"

"Look." I took out my phone, turned off the flashlight, and brought up the picture of Isaac in his vest. "It was in the Toronto *Metro*. The article was about a slot machine scam at Fallsview."

"Huh," Isaac said. "I didn't know I was in there. Okay, so what's all this about someone following you?"

"Well, after I saw the photo, I wanted to track you down so I could ask about Leonard. And why you lied to me. I talked to the head of security at the casino, who wouldn't tell me anything, but then this man started following me around. My friend here ended up following *him*, and she saw him go into a haunted house."

"Okay."

"The next day, I went over to the haunted house and asked the guy there about you. He wouldn't tell me anything at first, but eventually gave me a note. It said 'Roswell's 6 PM' on it."

"You were at the restaurant tonight."

"We were."

"Geez Louise."

"Who are these guys?" Patti asked. "Why are they following us? And how did they know where to find you?"

"I don't know why you were followed," Isaac said. "Although I'm getting the impression that the two of you might leap to wild conclusions now and then, so I'm not so sure you *were* followed. But you're talking about Mayhem Manor, right?"

"Yes," I said.

"My father owns that. He owns a lot of Clifton Hill. Whoever was working must have known about my dinner routine. Not sure why he told you, but okay."

"But the man from the casino did follow me. And he went right to your dad's haunted house."

"I don't know what to tell you."

The three of us stood in silence for a minute. I wanted to leave. Isaac had diffused the situation, yes. My suspicions had been somewhat quashed. But there was also an energy in the air that I didn't like. I needed to get outside.

I apologized—for breaking in, for stalking him, for casting suspicion on him. He said he understood. I offered to pay for the damages to his window and AC unit, but Isaac wouldn't let me. He said he had insurance and money in the bank, and anyway it was all a misunderstanding. I could tell Patti wanted out. Aside from the awkwardness of the situation, something about Isaac made me uncomfortable. Something in his eyes.

"I'm sorry about Leonard," Isaac said, opening the front door for us to leave. "He was a good man. I sure wish I could help you."

"Thank you," I said. "I'm so sorry about everything."

"It's fine. I understand."

Patti and I walked back to her car and Isaac disappeared inside the house. I sat down in the passenger seat and stared blankly at the glove compartment. We drove back down Maldon Road, toward the Captain's Inn.

"I grabbed this for you," Patti said. She took something out of her pocket and placed it on my lap. A cell phone.

"What the hell, Patti?"

"I found it in the closet in his office. Needs to be charged, but maybe you can find something on there."

"Jesus Christ. There's nothing to find. And you can't take his phone. We're lucky he didn't call the cops on us already. You know cell phones are like tracking devices, right? We need to be smart here. You need to return this."

"It's fine, don't worry. I was just trying to help. Anyway, I'm not going back there. That man gives me the creeps."

"Well mail it to him then." I handed back the phone. "Or destroy it. Just use your brain for once."

"Okay, I will. God. You know, you've changed, Colleen."

"I have?"

"Yeah. I can't tell if you've gotten worse or if I like you better."

I spent the night on the carpet at the foot of Patti's bed. I barely slept. Isaac had an answer for everything, but the answers weren't entirely satisfying. I didn't know anything about how AA worked, but it still seemed weird that Isaac had lied to me at the funeral. How had he known that Leonard died? What were those surveillance photos for? I should have said something, I thought. Maybe I was losing my mind, though. Allowing my grief to take over. Jumping to conspiratorial conclusions.

In the morning, I gathered my things. I walked Patti to her car—she had another shift at IHOP—and said goodbye. She gave me this apprehensive, borderline disgusted look when I leaned in for a hug, but she let me embrace her and even gave me a little pat on the back. I felt bad leaving her in Niagara Falls all alone, but it was time to go. I'd left Mother by herself long enough. I was already in debt. And I'd reached a dead end.

I called Mother on my walk to the bus depot. She answered on the first ring.

"You're really on your way?" she said.

"I'll be there in a few hours."

"I hope you had a nice vacation. I cleaned yesterday but you know how dusty this place gets. I should tidy up the couch-bed. I hope the place is nice for your return. I'll see what I can do before you get here. Oh, but it will have to do."

I boarded another double-decker and pulled out my screenplay notebook. The billboards, storage facilities, and water towers I passed were becoming familiar sights. I mostly kept my nose in my notebook. In my latest script idea, Mary Valentine learns to levitate. She uses this skill to spy through the second-floor windows of the boy's dormitory at Exley Riding School, gathering intel on Cameron Hawke, a new student with shifty behaviour. Cameron was up to something—I wasn't sure what that something would be just yet—and Mary was determined to suss out his plans. All I knew was that Mary would use her levitation powers to help her horse make the big final hurdle during the episode's climactic show-jumping scene. I would find my way there eventually. I had all the time in the world.

23

I settled back into life in Mimico. I went for brisk walks around the neighbourhood. I did push-ups on the rug beside my bed. I worked on a new *Riders of Exley* script. Mary Valentine's father is supposed to visit her at the riding school, but he never shows up. Mary spends all day waiting in the parking lot. She gets a nasty sunburn on her face and arms. Her father eventually calls and says he got tied up with business. She can hear that he's at a bar. She tells the other kids that her dad's an army medic and got called away to some foreign conflict, even though he's really an unemployed gambler. You never hear about Mary's father on the show, and I thought it would be an interesting avenue to explore. When I was Mary's age and people asked about my father, I always said he was an army medic and had to travel a lot. The other kids didn't need to know the real story—that he'd abandoned my family, and then died of alcohol poisoning. It was none of their business. If I just said he was in the army, we could move on and talk about something else. The script didn't go anywhere. I deleted it.

I regularly dropped in on *Reindeer Island* to see if Bonsai had any messages for me, but the island was deserted. I cruised the job boards for work. I couldn't bring myself to walk back into the call centre. It wasn't simply the embarrassment of returning after skipping out on so many shifts, after ducking so many calls from my supervisors. Although that was certainly a factor. I also couldn't picture myself back in that swivel chair, making calls. Conducting the same old surveys. Maybe it was time for a change—I could try office work or help out on film sets. Block traffic for the new Transformers movie. Wipe down the Transformers when it rained. Or I could see myself working security at a museum or high-end jewellery shop. Guarding an important door. Not a detective, obviously, but something in that realm.

Mother clung to me the first couple of days, biting at my heels, offering to make me tea at all hours. By the third day, however, she started spending more and more time locked in her room, playing harmonica along with the music channel. She sang backups on the choruses too. It sounded pretty good, through her door. I told her that it seemed like she had real musical talent, one night while we were eating crispy chicken and waffle fries in front of the TV.

"I'm just fooling around," she said. "But thank you, dear. I've been having a little fun I suppose. Actually, I've been meaning to tell you something."

"What?"

"Well, it's not a big deal. I don't know why I haven't told you yet. You're not mad, are you?"

"Mad about what?"

"Maybe it is a big deal. I don't know. You might get pretty mad. You're going to be just furious with me, Colleen."

"Just tell me. I'm sure it's fine."

"While you were away on your trip? Well, with the house empty, I thought I'd break out the harmonica and mess around a bit. But I wanted to play along to some real music. A lot of the stuff on the music channel is this new style that's hard to play along with. No real melody. The country channel's okay, but I don't like country so much. And you know how I am with the computer."

"Where are you going with this?"

"I got into Leonard's stuff, honey. I went through his records. And used his record player."

"Okay. And then what?"

"I played along with the albums. I felt awful the whole time though, I promise you. It was just the one time. I put everything back exactly where it was. I made sure of it."

"What happened?"

"What do you mean?".

"The thing you were scared to tell me is that you listened to Leonard's records?"

"Are you mad?"

"Of course not. You can listen to them anytime you want. Leonard isn't listening to them anymore. Why should they just sit there?"

"I thought you would be upset with me. That I went through his stuff."

"It's fine, honestly. Go nuts."

"Really? I wouldn't want to disturb his things if that upsets you. But there's this Eagles song I put on that one night. I came up with this neat melody and I'd love to try it again."

"Go right ahead. Honestly, it makes me happy to see you excited about this. I like hearing you play."

"Oh, I'm just fooling about."

Mother hurried through her dinner and then rushed off to fetch the record player and Eagles album from the corner of my room where Leonard's boxes sat. She put it on in her room and tooted along with her harmonica while I finished eating. I didn't mind Mother using Leonard's records one bit. It's odd how a person's possessions take on so much weight once they die. Leonard's Eagles album didn't mean squat to him when he was alive. Maybe at one time it did, but as long as I knew him, he didn't listen to records. They were just things he carted around from apartment to apartment, until he moved in with me. Most of my own possessions are meaningless.

My screenplay notebooks are pretty important, I suppose, and if I died someone could look through them and a sliver of my personality might poke through the pages. I like my pillows, but that's just because they're comfortable to sleep on. They're not significant life pillows. I have books that I read ages ago and then stuck on a shelf. I probably couldn't tell you two things about the plots of any of them. I have old pants and dresses and blouses that I don't wear, tucked away in the corner of the closet. Trinkets scattered along the windowsill. A wooden horse I found at the dollar store. A tiny box with nothing inside. Things that I have because I acquired them at one point and then forgot about them. They'd become invisible to me, just part of the shape of the room. But if I were to pass away suddenly, all these meaningless objects would come to represent me. Mother would hold the dollar store horse to her cheek and weep. I couldn't care less about that dumb horse.

Patti and I texted often. It was fun hearing about her days working at IHOP, looking for apartments, or the evenings she spent playing slots at the casino. I could picture everything she talked about because I'd been there. It was like I was still with her. I told her to keep an eye out for Isaac or the guys from the haunted house, but she didn't see anyone. No further run-ins with Dougie, either. One night she texted me about a particularly exciting episode of *Dateline* she was watching. She wanted me to watch it too, but I couldn't find it on the channels we had so she called me up and gave me a play-by-play.

"Oh my God," she said, "this woman was stabbed so many times the roommate who found her thought the body was a pile of laundry."

"I can't really hear this right now." I felt a lurch in my stomach with every detail she revealed. "Maybe we can talk tomorrow?"

"They think the guy who did it had military training. Can you imagine stabbing someone over and over again?"

"Please, Patti. I feel nauseous."

"Forty-eight stab wounds. That's insane. Try counting to forty-eight and imagine stabbing someone every second. That's what this guy did." ·

The episode eventually went to commercials and I got her to talk about IHOP instead. She said the tips were pretty good but that one of the managers had halitosis and was a bit condescending. He over-enunciated his words. Patti did this amazing impression of him and I giggled into the phone. I liked talking to Patti, once the *Dateline* stuff ended. We were like high school friends, chatting on the phone after dinner. It shows how you can never really know someone until you put in a solid effort. I'd known Patti for years and we'd never been so close. A wall had come down on our trip. The past few years my only real friend was Leonard. Besides Mother, of course. But then Leonard had all these secrets. I thought we were close, but now I wasn't so sure.

Patti and I said goodbye and I stepped into the shower. Without Patti to distract me, my mood turned sour. I couldn't get the water temperature right. Everything was annoying to me. I whipped the bar of soap at the wall and it dinged me in the shin. I cursed. I turned off the water and sat on the floor of the tub. What was Leonard doing in that bog? How had he got mixed up with dodgy Niagara Falls criminals and possibly the Russians? Did he have gambling debts? How was Isaac involved? I didn't trust him. But I'd reached a dead end. For the moment, at least, the way forward was unclear.

I couldn't give up hope. I stood up and turned the water back on. So it was a little cold, big deal. I'd be fine. I just needed to keep my head on straight, find a new job, take care of Mother, finish my script, figure out my life, and soon enough I'd have my answers. The universe reveals its secrets to those who are patient. I read that in a fortune cookie once and put the little slip of paper in my wallet. I lost the slip, but the words remain true.

24

One morning, I awoke to find a map on the kitchen table. A building map, hand-drawn in blue pen, with the different sections and rooms labelled. I recognized Leonard's handwriting instantly. At the top of the page, he'd written "South West Detention Centre."

I knocked on Mother's door and she called me in. She was sitting up in bed, watching *Ellen*.

"What is this?" I asked, holding up the map.

"I found it tucked into the sleeve of *Making Movies*."

"*Making Movies*?"

"Sorry, it's by the group Dire Straits. One of Leonard's records. I put it out for you in case it might be interesting. I didn't mean to pry."

I took the map back to the kitchen table and sat down. Leonard had drawn a map of a prison and then hidden it in one of his record sleeves. He drew the parking lots, the cafeteria. All the exits were labelled. The guard towers. Leonard had worked a few construction jobs in the past. Perhaps it was just a work thing. But then why did he keep it? Why would he need to draw the map himself? I Googled "South West Detention Centre." The prison was in Windsor. Leonard had never lived in Windsor, as far as I knew. I stuck the map in my screenplay notebook.

I turned the kettle on for tea and put a corn muffin from the fridge on a plate. While I waited for the water to boil, I thought about the prison map. What else had Leonard hidden around the house? I wondered. There could be other secret maps, notes, maybe even a diary. Something that might shed light on what had happened to him.

I started with Leonard's box of records. There were only twenty or so albums. I pulled each record from its sleeve and waited for loose papers to fall out, but other than a few lyric sheets nothing surfaced. Then I moved on to his clothes. I checked the pockets of his jeans, his jackets, his cargo shorts. There was an old bus transfer in one pocket, a loose cough drop in another. But no notes. I rifled through all his boxes, checked the toes of his shoes. Nothing.

I went out to the driveway and got into Leonard's Toyota Yaris. I'd looked through it once before, when the police brought it back to the house, but at the time I wasn't looking with purpose. I'd just popped the glove compartment, checked the trunk. This time, however, I'd be exhaustive in my efforts. I rifled under the seats—I found a flattened Smarties box and one Smartie. I took everything out of the glove box. I checked between the pages of the owner's manual and even looked inside the battery compartment of Leonard's flashlight. Then I opened the trunk. Spare tire, two cloth shopping bags, and a bag of socks Leonard had been meaning to return because they turned out to be child's size. I pulled everything out onto the driveway and even shook the tire, as if a revelatory note would flutter to my feet. Looking inside the empty trunk, I noticed that the lining was ripped along the left side. It was taped down.

I pulled the lining back—it came up much too easily once the tape had been removed—and noticed that, oddly, the floor of the trunk was made of wood. There was a rectangular hatch cut into the wood about the size of a microwave door. I pried the hatch open with my keys and set the thin rectangle of wood aside. Something gleamed in the darkness below. Leonard had constructed a false wooden bottom and placed it in the trunk, creating a secret compartment.

I used the flashlight on my phone to illuminate the secret compartment. The first thing I noticed was a small black carrying case. I pulled it out, set it aside. Heavy for its size. I leaned into the trunk, reached around in the hole, and pulled up a brown folder, a map, and a canister of bear spray. What the hell was Leonard doing with bear spray? I thought. More importantly, why was he hiding it? I opened the black carrying case. Inside, set in a layer of black foam, was a handgun.

I snapped the case shut and set it inside the trunk. I spun around and looked out at the street. No one was around. No one had seen the gun. As far as I could tell, anyway. Leonard had a goddamn handgun. Stashed in our trunk. There's no way it was legal. He really was into something deep. I put the case and the bear spray back into the secret compartment, then replaced the little wooden door. Folded the lining back and reset the tape. I returned the tire, the shopping bags, and the socks to the trunk and closed the lid. I took the map and brown folder inside the house with me.

Grabbing the corn muffin from the plate I'd set out earlier, I went into my room and locked the door. First, I unfolded the map and laid it out on my bed.

Morrison Bog.

This one wasn't hand drawn like the prison map. It looked like a computer printout. On a large piece of paper, the size of a road map. Leonard must have had it done at Kinko's. Or maybe it came from the library. There it was, all laid out. Morrison Bog, the site of my husband's death. There was a circle on the map drawn with black marker. It looked to be right about where Leonard's body was found.

A moan squeezed itself out of my throat. I started crying. My mouth was full of corn muffin and I spit crumbs out onto the map. I pushed the map off the bed and lay down face-first on my comforter. Drooling muffin paste onto the bed. Moaning, crying. I couldn't stop myself. It didn't make any sense. What was Leonard doing? It was like he had planned everything. Like he knew all along he was going to drive out to that exact spot and kill himself. He didn't say a thing to me, just went ahead with his secret plans. No note. Left me completely in the dark.

Unless, I thought, the black circle on the map was a meet-up spot. Maybe he did have gambling debts and the criminals he owed had given him a deadline and a location to complete the transaction. They wanted him to drive out to a remote, wooded area with an envelope of money and settle the matter in secret. And poor, naïve Leonard went.

I sat up, opened the brown envelope. The cash he was supposed to hand over to the casino goons, I figured. It wasn't cash, however, but a stack of receipts. Nearly an inch thick, tied together with a rubber band. The first was from a Walmart in St. Catharines, dated March tenth:

2L Pepsi ×12
Nestle Water 12Pack
Gravol Tablets ×2
PC Pape Towels 6Pack ×2

Another was from a St. Catharines No Frills, January twenty-second:

Chick Peas ×10
Bean Medley ×10
Kidney Bean ×10
Nestle Water 12Pack
PC Ginger Ale ×2
PC Toilet Paper 12Pack ×3

Another came from a Canadian Tire in Hamilton, November nineteenth:

HMK L-Handle Shovel
Black & Decker 20V Max Li-Ion Cordless Drill & Circular Saw
Combo Kit
PVC Coated Garden Gloves

There were a few more like this, from various dates. Why did Leonard purchase these items? Why did he hide the receipts? Food supplies, cleaning supplies, tools. He hadn't brought these things back home. Most of the receipts were for gas. He'd filled up at several stations along the route to Niagara Falls, or Morrison Bog. One of the stations, just outside of St. Catharines, he'd been to six times. The oldest receipt in the stack, for a fill-up in Grimsby, dated back to the previous July. Leonard had been living this secret life for at least a year.

I put the bog map and the receipts into my screenplay notebook with the prison map and went to the bathroom. Washed my face, drank a few mouthfuls of lukewarm water from the tap. Sat down on the toilet. I could hear Mother playing harmonica through the wall. A record playing in the background. The Beach Boys. *All Summer Long.* Mother was off key. I turned the tap back on and let the water run noisily down the drain.

The gun in the black case wouldn't leave my mind. I'd try and watch TV but all I could see was the gun, floating in front of the screen. It seemed like the proper thing to do would be to phone the police. Let them deal with it. But my investigation seemed to be shaping into something again. I had more evidence. Maybe I needed to go back to Niagara Falls. I couldn't let the cops mess everything up. They didn't care about Leonard. They'd get Isaac and the casino men and the Russians up on their heels and my search would end there. Besides, who knows, I could end up in trouble over the gun. They could even blame me for shooting Leonard. Probably not, but the point is that I wasn't sure what to do—only that I needed to do something.

I called Patti. She didn't answer. She was probably at work. I texted her to call me back ASAP. I watched TV with Mother. *Along Came Polly* was playing. Mother flicked between that and a dating show. I wasn't paying attention. I fell asleep for a while. When I woke up, Mother was asleep too. She'd been eating a sandwich and there was a big piece of lettuce on her neck. No missed calls.

Patti didn't end up calling back until around seven-thirty that evening. I was a ball of nerves by that point, worried about what I'd discovered in Leonard's trunk, but also worried about Patti. Dougie could've done something, I thought. But she was fine. She'd worked a double shift. I let her unload some work stress by listening to her IHOP horror stories for a minute or two, and then I cut in with my news. I told her about the gun, the receipts, the maps.

"There was actually a *Dateline* about this kind of thing a while ago," Patti said. "The killer even had bear spray. This is crazy."

"Leonard wasn't a killer," I said.

"But the real score here is the receipts. You know what you should do? Drive down to Niagara Falls tomorrow. You can stop at all those places along the way. The gas stations. The Canadian Tire. Show the cashiers a picture of Leonard and see if they recognize him. You never know, maybe he told them something. Maybe they saw something."

"I guess I could take Leonard's car."

"There you go, you can take Leonard's car. I'd get rid of the gun first."

"I can put it under the porch or something."

"Exactly. You put the gun under the porch, you drive down here, you flash Leonard's photo around along the way. I'm working until noon, so you can come for then. Pick me up at work. I'll have a stack of pancakes waiting for you. God, this is really ramping up. I thought it would be because of Isaac's phone, but I guess that was a dead end. Good thing your mom found that map."

"I know," I said. "She saved the investigation. By the way, what did you end up doing with the phone? Did you mail it to him anonymously?"

"Are you being serious?" Patti said.

"Yeah, what did you do with it?"

"Colleen, I put it in your bag. You didn't find it?"

"You what?"

"At the hotel, before you left. I put Isaac's phone in your backpack. You were saying that we'd hit this dead end. I thought there could be something on the phone that would help you figure out where to look next."

"I told you to get rid of it! Jesus Christ, I have Isaac's phone in my house, right now?"

"I assumed you already looked through it and didn't find anything."

"I need to take it somewhere. Shit. What if Isaac went to the police and they've tracked it to my house?"

"The cops have more important things to do than look for lost phones. Anyway, you can get rid of it when you come down tomorrow. You've had it this long. You should charge it up and see what's on there before you leave."

"I can't do that."

"Why not?"

"I don't know. I guess I can. Shit. Okay, I should go."

"I'll see you tomorrow?"

"I'll see you tomorrow."

I hung up and retrieved my backpack from the closet. Sure enough, Isaac's cell phone was tucked away in the bottom. An older model with physical buttons below the screen. The battery was dead. My phone's charger didn't fit, but Mother's did. I plugged it in and a battery icon popped up on screen, with a little lightning bolt to show that it was charging up. I tried every button, but I couldn't figure out a way to navigate away from this screen and look through the contents of the phone. I'd have to wait, it seemed. In the meantime, I loaded up *Reindeer Island.*

Heartsong stood on the beach, looking out across the water. Small waves lapped against the shore in the moonlight. Where is this island supposed to be? I thought. Somewhere tropical, obviously. But was it on Earth? Or some Mormon planet? Maybe another dimension. The afterlife.

Heartsong trotted up the beach and passed through the ivory archway into Kolob Village. A glowing stream of green water snaked its way through the village and Heartsong had to cross several quaint footbridges. All was quiet. I had been wandering around *Reindeer Island* for a few minutes now and had yet to cross paths with another player. I wanted to find Bonsai—maybe he had another message for me.

Heartsong entered the village square, where a golden reindeer statue stood tall. The statue's legs shot up like California redwood trees, its head like a small house. It really was beautiful. Like an interactive painting or a lucid dream. It wasn't breathtaking the way Horseshoe Falls was breathtaking, but it also kind of was. A similar feeling came over me. The world was beautiful and had meaning in it. Even if I was looking at pixels on a screen, put there by a religious game designer. Those pixels were still a real part of the world, and they were still beautiful. I wondered if Leonard had stood in the same spot, looking up and admiring the enormous statue. He must have. I felt so close to him in moments like this, living out experiences he had lived. Like seeing the home your grandmother grew up in for the first time—you picture what it was like for your grandmother, running around the yard in her galoshes, all tiny, in another era, and your understanding deepens.

I stared into the screen, a confusing medley of joy and heartbreak tumbling around in my stomach, when Isaac's phone buzzed in the corner of the room. I shut the laptop lid and went over. The phone's home screen was up now. I opened Isaac's contact list, wondering if Leonard was in there, but there weren't any contacts at all. The call history was blank too. No text messages, no social media apps. No photos. It seemed like the phone had never been used, which was odd, because it was so old. The only thing I could find on it was a video file. About four minutes in length. I opened it up.

The filmmaker was walking through a forest. A faint light streamed in through the trees. You could hear twigs snapping—they weren't following any sort of path or trail. The frame bounced up and down with each step. The filmmaker stopped walking and began to speak, off-screen.

"We're here," the voice said. "Look at the tree with the big knot in the trunk."

It was Leonard's voice.

I paused the video. Scrubbed back to the beginning, watched the camera bob through the woods again.

"We're here. Look at the tree with the big knot in the trunk."

I paused the video again. My husband had recorded this footage. But why? And why did Isaac have it on his phone? Unless it was actually Leonard's phone—a burner. Like drug dealers have on TV shows, and probably in real life too. Isaac could have killed Leonard and then taken it from Leonard's pocket. It was shocking to hear his voice again. I didn't have any recordings of him to listen to after his passing. He mumbled his name if you called his voicemail. I'd tried that a few times, but it didn't provide much satisfaction. Now I had full sentences. My Leonard—it was like he was in the room with me. I began to cry. I started coughing. I clicked back to the start of the video again. I'd let it play through this time.

"We're here. Look at the tree with the big knot in the trunk. A few metres back and just to the right is the door. Let's go."

The camera pushed forward again, past the tree and to the right. Panned down. A hand—Leonard's hand, wearing a brown glove— reached down into a patch of grass. The hand darted around on the ground, searching for something. Leonard pulled up the grass, along a seam. It was like a carpet. Leonard peeled back the grass, revealing a plank of wood. A metal latch was fixed to the side of the plank, which Leonard slid open.

"I need two hands for this," he said.

The camera was placed on the ground. I was looking up at a canopy of pine trees. A distorted creaking came through the phone's tiny speaker, followed by a thud. Leonard picked the camera up and pointed it back at the spot on the ground. Where the grass carpet had been peeled back, there was a square opening in the ground. About the size of my TV. The wooden plank was a door, on hinges, now open. It lay atop the grass carpet on the far side of the opening.

"There she is," Leonard said, the camera pointed at the hole. I could see the faint outline of a ladder reaching down into the darkness. "Still a few months away, but I wanted you to see. Should give you an idea. Let's go down."

The camera spun around quickly and then went dark. Some distorted noises, like the microphone was scraping against some- thing. He'd put his phone in his pocket while he climbed into the hole, I assumed. Nothing happened for a good ten seconds. I stared at the dark screen, wiping tears from my eyes. None of what I'd seen so far made sense.

A light came on and the camera adjusted. I was looking at wooden shelves stacked with canned goods. Two-litre bottles of Pepsi. Packs of water bottles covered in plastic wrap. Leonard's warped shadow twisted across the various packages and cans.

"Alright, so we've got some storage here right when you climb down. There's lots of space up by the generator, which you'll see later. But let's move over to the other room and I'll show you what still needs to be done."

The camera turned and pointed up the ladder for a second, to where Leonard had just climbed down. It looked like he'd closed the hatch door. The camera turned back down to the shelves and panned over to show a narrow hallway. Light bulbs were attached to wooden beams at either end.

"You'll have to duck here. You'll get used to it." The camera weaved through the narrow hallway, entered another small room. Leonard reached up and turned on a light. Another supply shelf. Buckets and plastic garbage bags strewn about. Then the camera turned and focused on a bench, attached to the left wall. "This will be your bunk. Might be a tight fit, but you're probably used to that by now. And I can put up a shower curtain for privacy. You don't get that up at South West. Okay now, check this out."

The camera panned to the opposite wall. A bedsheet hung from the corners—one of Mother's bedsheets. With the wildflower pattern. Leonard reached forward and pulled the sheet back. A gun rack was built into the wall. Three guns rested there: Leonard's father's hunting rifle, which I recognized. An old shotgun I'd never seen before. Then some kind of assault weapon. Like they used in the military. It was massive.

"A good start, no? Still lots to do, but you get the idea. There's about a thousand pounds of supplies left and I'm averaging about a hundred pounds a week. A few runs to go and then I need to reinforce some of the beams. I'll run a safety check before you get out here. More storage and the generator upstairs, but that still needs work. You can see that later. So that's pretty much where we're at."

The video cut off there.

I barely slept. I forced myself to lie atop the comforter on my bed for a few hours, but I kept waking up panicked. My sleep T-shirt soaked with sweat. I must have watched the video fifty times that night.

Somewhere in the middle of watching Leonard's bunker video over and over again, I'd retrieved the map of Morrison Bog from my screenplay notebook. I stared at the black circle, drawn near the spot where Leonard's body had been found. Maybe it wasn't a meet-up location. Maybe it marked the location of the bunker. The secret hatch, where you pull up the grass and climb down a ladder into Leonard's hideout. The cops hadn't found it, or else they would have told me. I needed to go down there. That's where my answers lay. I was heading to Niagara Falls the next day already. When I called Patti to tell her about the video, she agreed—in the morning, I'd drive to Patti's IHOP, pick her up, and then we'd head straight for the bog.

Another detail from the video that haunted me that night, as I lay atop my blanket, thoughts spiralling in the darkness, was Leonard's mention of South West.

"I can put up a shower curtain for privacy," he said, the camera pointed at the small bunk. "You don't get that up at South West."

The hand-drawn map Mother found in Leonard's Dire Straits record was for the South West Detention Centre in Windsor. Leonard had made the video for an ex-con. He was planning to bring some prisoner, some criminal to his hideout in the woods. Like one of the Russian scammers. Perhaps the man being led away by the cops in the *Metro* photograph. It could be Leonard's killer. And they might still be down there. I'd have to be careful. But whoever it was and whatever Leonard had gotten himself caught up in, the truth lay beneath the ground over in Morrison Bog. Part of me wanted to leave right away, in the middle of the night. Drive out there immediately with a flashlight and find the secret door. Put an end to the whole thing. But I didn't want to worry Mother by disappearing in the night and I needed at least a few hours of sleep. Leonard's bunker would be waiting for me the next day. Unoccupied, I hoped.

In the morning, I made toast and tea for Mother and me. We sat in front of the TV. *Along Came Polly* was on again. *Along Came Polly* was always on.

"So, I talked to Patti last night," I said. "She wants me to come help her with the apartment search. Is it okay if I drive over there today? I'll come back tonight. Tomorrow at the latest."

"You're sure spending a lot of time in Niagara Falls," Mother said.

"Is that a problem?"

"No, I was—"

"Because it's really none of your business. So what if I'm spending some time away? I never go anywhere."

"I didn't mean it like that."

"What did you mean then? I'm an adult for Christ's sake. I can't sit around here babysitting you twenty-four-seven. It's ridiculous."

"Oh, Colleen," Mother said. She put her head down to her chest. A tear streaked down her cheek. She began to rock back and forth in her chair.

"I'm not falling for this," I said. I stared her down. Chomping a piece of toast. "You can't be all judgmental and then act like the victim. Hell, no."

Mother continued to convulse slightly in her chair. Spittle on her chin. I stood up from the couch and stomped into my bedroom to pack.

"I'll be back tonight," I shouted through my closed door. "Tomorrow at the latest. You'll be fine." I stuffed the same jeans, T-shirts, shorts, and other clothing that I'd taken on prior trips into my backpack, as well as my screenplay notebook, which had Leonard's maps and receipts tucked between the pages.

I went down the hall and found a zebra-striped gift bag in Mother's craft cupboard. I took this out to the driveway and opened Leonard's trunk. Pulled back the lining, opened the secret compartment with my keys. Placed the gun case and bear spray into the gift bag, then replaced the false bottom and lining. I slid the gift bag under my bed. I'd deal with the gun later, bring it to the police station. After I'd finished with my investigation.

"Anyway, will you be alright?" I said, returning to the living room, backpack slung over my shoulder, Leonard's car keys squeezed inside my fist.

Mother's chair was empty.

"Mother?" I walked over to her bedroom, but it was empty. I checked her closet. She wasn't in the bathtub. She wasn't in the laundry room. All her usual hiding spots were empty. And then I spotted her white bathrobe out the kitchen window. Mother was in the backyard, standing on her tiptoes, peering over the fence. I went outside.

"What are you doing?"

"I've done something silly, Colleen. I'm too stupid for this world."

"I'm sorry, Mother. It's okay. I didn't mean to snap at you."

"No, I threw my harmonica over the fence. I think it's under that white van."

I walked up to the fence and looked over into The Blue Drop's parking lot. A white van was parked by the dumpster.

"Why would you go and do that?"

"I was upset with myself for what I said."

"You didn't say anything. I'm sorry, Mother. I was taking something out on you that had nothing to do with you."

"Well, I'm sorry anyway. When are you leaving?"

"Let's go get your harmonica. And then I'm leaving."

We couldn't find the harmonica, after twenty minutes of searching. Mother wanted to purchase a new one right away, so I made sure she had cab fare and then dropped her off at a music shop on my way out of the city.

I made my way through Mimico traffic, out onto the highway. I switched on the radio and nodded along to a Rihanna song. An abrasive commercial came on after and I changed stations until I found a classic rock one. I didn't know what Dire Straits sounded like but the band playing seemed like they could be Dire Straits. I drummed my fingers on the steering wheel. I didn't have to listen to horrible school shooting stories. I was in control now.

I took the same route as the bus. I recognized scenes from my previous trips: a blank billboard in Burlington; an auto dealer with a hunched over, sickly looking inflatable pigeon on the roof; bridge graffiti near Hamilton that said, FUCK MAGIC.

It did feel strange, driving Leonard's car again. Like playing his character in *Reindeer Island*. It was as if part of him was still alive. As if his spirit was inside of me as I pressed down on the gas and changed lanes. Or maybe his spirit was in the car itself. I don't know, it was more of a weird feeling than a well-thought-out theory.

I found the gas station outside of St. Catharines where Leonard had stopped six times, according to his receipts. I needed to fuel up anyway. When I went inside to pay, I opened a photo of Leonard on my phone. The Denny's birthday photo. I showed it to the cashier.

"Do you recognize this man?"

The cashier squinted at my phone.

"Who are you?" he said.

"Does that mean you've seen him before?"

"No, it means I'm asking who you are."

"I'm Annie."

"I mean, are you police?"

"No."

"Then who are you?"

"I just told you. I'm Annie."

"Who the hell is Annie?"

"I'm Annie."

"I know that, but are you with the police?"

"I already said that I'm not."

"Okay, but then who are you?"

I snatched my phone away and left. It didn't matter if that idiot saw Leonard anyway, I knew. Everything I needed would be inside the bunker.

When I finally reached Niagara Falls, I drove straight to Patti's IHOP. I texted her from the parking lot. She immediately called.

"I'm at the hotel," she said. "I had to leave early. Dougie stopped by the restaurant again."

"He's still here? What happened?"

"He's deranged. Nothing happened. I saw him walk up to the front doors before he could spot me. I ducked out the back and took a cab here. I can't keep doing this. I'm gonna get fired."

"They'd have to be insane to fire you. Don't worry. I'll be right over."

"Just keep an eye out for Dougie."

I drove to the Captain's Inn but parked behind a campervan at the hotel across the street in case Dougie somehow recognized Leonard's car. I walked over and up to Patti's room. She answered the door in her IHOP shirt. It felt so good to see her again. We'd been through something together. I wrapped my arms around her and she went stiff. I didn't care.

"You didn't see Dougie?" Patti sat on the bed and turned the TV volume down. Cellphone footage of 9/11. The twin towers smoking, crowds scrambling.

"All clear." I sat down at the little wooden desk next to the TV. A wet towel hung over the back of the chair, so I had to lean forward.

"Let's see this video," Patti said. I loaded it up and handed her the phone. She stared in wide-eyed disbelief.

"This is fucking crazy," she said. "That's Leonard?"

"Yes, that's him filming."

"This is insane. He made an underground fort in the woods. So where is this?"

"I'm pretty sure it's in Morrison Bog. Near where his body was found. Check this out."

I showed Patti the map of the bog with the black circle.

"What if someone's living down there?" Patti said. "With all those guns. This could be dangerous."

"I doubt there's anyone in there now. We'll just have to be careful. We'll open the door quietly and listen. We'll call something out before we go down. I don't know. There's probably nobody in there."

"I feel like I'm on *Dateline*."

"This is serious, Patti."

"So is *Dateline*."

Patti changed out of her work clothes, and we walked across the street to my car. Patti wanted to drive but I insisted on taking us there myself. This was my mission. I let her play with the radio.

We drove south. It was about a half hour away from Niagara Falls. I'd never been to Morrison Bog before. I'd thought about visiting after Leonard died. Maybe it would help with the grieving process to see the actual place where he was found, I thought, but I ultimately decided against it. The bog had nothing to do with Leonard's life. That's what I cared about—my living husband. The memories we shared, his laugh. Not his grim demise. No thank you. But now, after all that I'd learned over the past few weeks, a trip to Morrison Bog was necessary.

"You see that black Honda Civic a few cars back?" Patti said. We were just outside of Welland. I looked in the rear-view.

"Yeah?"

"It's been back there for a while now. I saw it as we were leaving."

"You think it's following us?"

"I don't know, maybe."

"I'm sure it's fine. Here, I'll stop at the Wendy's up ahead. We'll see if they stop too."

We pulled into the lot outside of Wendy's and watched the black Civic drive on.

"There," I said. I clapped my hands together. "It's gone. All good."

Patti seemed satisfied, but now my mind started racing. What if someone *was* trying to follow us? Like one of the guys from Mayhem Manor, or some Russian operative. An ex-con with a cache of weapons piled up on the passenger seat. Regardless, the black car was gone. I pulled back out onto the highway and continued on toward the bog. I checked my mirror every few minutes, but no one seemed to be following us. The black car didn't resurface. Still, I gripped the steering wheel like I was hanging from a ledge.

We pulled off the highway and parked on the same service road where the police had found Leonard's car. The road was lined with dense forest on both sides. No other vehicles in sight. I took out the map of the bog and figured out where we were in relation to the black circle.

"Should be about a twenty-minute hike," I said.

"You can't park any closer?"

"This is the closest spot."

"It looks like where a serial killer would take his victims to finish them off."

"Patti!"

"I don't mean that's what happened with Leonard. It just reminds me of when a girl gets into a stranger's car in a movie, and then she realizes the guy's going the wrong way and they end up in a place like this. I'm not talking about Leonard."

We stepped out of the car and started walking into the bush. Mosquitoes and flies buzzed around our heads. There wasn't a path, as far as I could tell. In the distance, however, through the trees, I could see the edge of a large pond. Once we walked around to the northern tip of the pond, the place circled on Leonard's map would be half a kilometre to the east.

"Hold on," Patti said. We were about twenty feet from the road. She put her hand to her ear.

"What?" I said, but immediately heard what she was referring to. A vehicle coming down the service road.

"Stand behind a tree," Patti said. "Just in case."

I stood behind a tree.

A few seconds later, a car glided into view. A black Honda Civic. The car we'd lost at the Wendy's. It slowed down, then pulled up behind Leonard's car. I looked over at Patti, peering out from behind her own tree. The driver stepped out of the vehicle and slammed the door. It was Dougie. He walked over to Leonard's car and looked in the driver's window.

"Patti," I whispered.

She looked over at me.

"Run," she said.

It didn't strike me as the brightest plan—if we stayed hidden, Dougie surely wouldn't see us there—but Patti was already tearing through the brush. I ran after her.

Twigs and leaves smacked my face. The ground was either slippery with mud or clogged with tree roots, foliage, and forest debris, but Patti and I pressed on. The sun wasn't beating down on us like it had been on the road, but the forest air was muggy and thick. It felt like I was being boiled in a bag. I turned my head back a few times but didn't see Dougie. I couldn't tell if he'd heard us run off and had been following us through the bog, or if he'd already given up and driven away. Best to put some distance between us and the road first, then ask that question. We ran out onto a rough path as we closed in on the pond.

"Go left," I shouted ahead to Patti. We turned left and ran up the path.

When we reached the northern shore of the pond, I noticed a small thicket of pine trees up ahead, beside the path. I yelped to get Patti's attention and pointed to the thicket. She got the idea, and we ran and hid underneath one of the pines. You wouldn't see us through the boughs of pine needles unless you were really looking for us there, but we could see out. We watched the path, caught our breath.

"That was Dougie," Patti whispered.

"I know."

"Whose car was he driving?"

"I don't know."

"Do you think he saw us?"

"I don't know."

"Fuck."

"I know."

We waited in silence for ten or so minutes. No sign of Dougie. Cautiously, we climbed out from under the pine and walked east. I led the way this time. Toward the bunker, I hoped. We stepped carefully, avoiding twigs when we could. Listening for Dougie. Looking over our shoulders. Ignoring the flies and mosquitoes.

The path disappeared and we continued through the bush. I knew what to look for: The entrance to Leonard's bunker was at the bottom of an incline. I could see the trees sloping upward in the distance, to our left. Once we reached the bottom of the hill, I needed to find the tree with the big knot in the trunk from Leonard's video.

As we moved through the forest, it dawned on me where I was. Near the site of Leonard's death. This is where he spent his last moments, I thought. I might be stepping on the exact spot on the ground where he drew his final breath. I slowed down. Patti bumped into me.

"Sorry," I said, turning around. "I was thinking about how Leonard—"

"Just go!" Patti said.

Patti spotted the tree with the knot before I did. Once we reached the incline, I'd been scanning each tree but somehow missed it. Patti whistled and pointed. We walked up the hill to the tree with the knot, continued up a few feet farther and just to the right of the tree, then panned our heads down, like the camera had. There was the patch of grass.

I got down on my knees and stuck my hands into the grass. I felt around until I found the edge of the carpet, then pulled it back. Just like Leonard had done. There was the wooden door to the bunker.

"This is it," I said. "Jesus. You don't think there's someone down there, do you?"

"I don't know," Patti said. "Maybe this is a bad idea."

Just then, a loud snap sounded behind us. Patti yelped. We turned around.

Dougie lay on the ground in the near distance, clutching his knee. Maybe fifty feet away. In the dense brush. It looked like he had tripped over something. He'd tracked us somehow.

"Goddamnit." Dougie began to pull himself up.

"Help me with the door," I said. I slid open the latch. "We can lock ourselves in."

The door to the bunker was heavier than expected. A dense, thick slab of wood reinforced with metal strips along the bottom. Patti and I managed it together though. The bunker was completely dark, which made it seem more likely that it was unoccupied. Patti slipped down the ladder first. Dougie was barrelling right for us. A crazed expression on his face. I propped the door up on my shoulders and manoeuvred down the ladder. The door slid back into place.

There was a large metal handle screwed onto the underside of the door. I pulled the handle toward me with one hand and took my phone out of my pocket with the other. Using my phone's flashlight, I scanned the wooden plank above me—there was no lock. I'd have to keep pulling on the handle to stop Dougie from getting in.

"Patti," I called down. "There's no lock. Can you try and squeeze up here with me? Help me hold the door shut."

"Okay. Shit. Did he see us go in here?"

"He did."

Patti's hands grabbed at my shoes. I pushed myself against the dirt wall and Patti squirmed up beside me. I was spooning her. My sweaty chest pressed into her sweaty back. I guided her hands up to the metal handle and she gripped it alongside my hands.

Muted footsteps approached overhead. Dougie pounded on the door above us. The knocking echoed down into the hole. He started pulling at the door. Patti and I held on tight. We could feel the wood shift a little, but he wouldn't be able to pull it open. Not with the two of us holding it shut anyway. We'd have to hang on. How long before Dougie gave up and left was unclear, however.

"Patti!" Dougie shouted through the door. His voice was muffled and watery, but we could make out what he was saying. "What the hell are you doing in there? Open up. We need to talk."

Patti didn't respond. I kept quiet. Dougie let go of the door and pounded on it again.

"What the hell are you doing in there?" Dougie shouted. "Let me in."

"Don't let go," Patti whispered.

"I won't," I whispered back. "Maybe one of us can climb down and get one of the guns."

"No. Don't let go. Don't leave me."

Dougie yanked the door again. We held on tight.

I'd made it to Leonard's underground hideout and here I was stuck on a ladder, holding a door shut. I wanted to kill Dougie. The idea of climbing down and retrieving one of Leonard's guns was simply to scare him off, but part of me wanted to pop open the hatch and shoot him right in the chest. In the face. He was ruining everything. What was he planning to do with Patti anyway, if we did come out of the hole? Reason with her? He was insane. He might kill her—he might kill me too. He deserved to get shot. Dougie should have been the one who died in the woods, not my husband. But I didn't budge. I held on with Patti while Dougie pounded and pulled at the door. My arms were already sore. My back ached too. But I didn't let go of the handle.

After a few minutes, Dougie gave up trying to open the door. No more knocking. All was quiet above us. Quiet inside the bunker too. Patti and I remained silent, listening. There were no sounds of footsteps walking away. Dougie was still there, directly above us.

A memory from The Farm snapped into place in my mind. I was in the dark basement. The middle of the night. I was asleep and then someone crawled into my bunk next to me.

"It's me," the intruder said. I recognized the voice as a fifteen-year-old girl who had moved down to Moon Camp that day. "I need to sleep in your bed with you."

She smelled awful. Like she hadn't showered in months. Like she'd shit herself.

"Go back to your bed," I said. "You can't sleep here."

"No," she said. She wrapped her pungent arms around me, gripped me close. "I need to be here."

"Get off me," I said. I tried to push her away, but she was stronger than me. I felt like I was going to throw up.

She started crying. I relaxed my body a little. She didn't loosen her grip. I breathed through my mouth. Eventually, morning would come, I knew. At some point, I managed to fall asleep. I awoke a few hours later and the girl was gone. Her stench still lingered, but she was back in her own bed. Or nestled up against someone else, testing their endurance.

This memory flashed in my mind in an instant. Like most of my Citizens of Light memories, I'd blocked it out. I hadn't thought of that poor girl since I'd left Woodbine's property. I wanted out of that hole in the ground. As much as I wanted to investigate Leonard's bunker, I needed to be back on top of the earth. Back in the light. Out of the forest, too. I wanted to be home with Mother. On the front steps of Mother's home with a Pepsi, watching squirrels dart around the yard.

"Hey," Dougie said. I was startled by his voice—he'd been silent for a few minutes. "Who are you?"

A faint voice responded, just a murmur. Someone else was up there with him.

"This is none of your business," Dougie said. "Move the fuck along."

The second voice sounded closer now, a little more distinct. A man's voice. He said something about the door.

"Take it easy," Dougie said. "I don't want any trouble."

Footsteps above us. The two men were still talking, but it was quieter, too muffled to discern. Then there were two explosive pops—it sounded like a gun going off. Incredibly loud. I felt Patti's body trembling next to me on the ladder. Scuffling sounds, which seemed to move away from the door, into the distance. An eerie silence above us now.

"What the hell?" I whispered.

"I'm scared, Colleen," Patti said.

I took my right hand off the handle and placed it on her shoulder.

"It's okay. Maybe we're dreaming."

A minute later, footsteps approached the bunker door. Someone knocked again, but in a more polite way. Three distinct knocks.

"Come on out," a man's muffled voice said. Not Dougie's. "It's safe. I'm a police officer."

He didn't pull at the door.

"Should we go up?" Patti whispered.

"I don't know. Do you think he's really a cop?"

"Oh yeah. Shit. Maybe he's not."

"Come on now," the man called down. "Open up or we're coming down." He knocked again, three more times.

"I think we have to," Patti said.

I nodded, even though Patti couldn't see me. I let go of the handle. We started pushing open the door. Light poured in. A man kneeled before the hole above us. He wore a ski mask. A pistol in his hands.

2 8

Patti climbed out of the hole first. The man in the ski mask had flipped the bunker door back on its hinges and then directed Patti to sit on the ground a few feet away. I started climbing out too, when the man stopped me.

"Hold on there," he said. His voice sounded familiar. He wore a short-sleeved plaid shirt tucked into black jeans. Black work boots. "I need you to help me with something."

"Okay," I said. I didn't see Dougie anywhere.

"Give me your phones," the man in the ski mask said.

We handed him our phones and he put them in his pocket.

"Great," the man said. He pulled his mask off, revealing a flushed, sweaty, but recognizable face.

"Isaac," I said.

"Nice to see you two again," Isaac said.

"What are you doing here? Were you following us?"

"Looks like I wasn't the only one. Who the heck was that moron?"

"Where is he?" Patti said. "What did you do with Dougie?"

"Keep your voice down, for Pete's sake," Isaac said, pointing his gun at Patti's chest. "Dougie, you said? So, you two do know him. Who's Dougie? And how'd you find this place?"

"What did you do?" Patti said.

"He's fine," Isaac said. "But you'll need to lower your voice. I will shoot you if I have to. That's a guarantee."

"Isaac, please," I said. "Dougie is Patti's husband. You're sure he's okay? We heard gunshots."

"Don't you worry about it," Isaac said. "Now listen. I've got a job for you. I need you to climb back down the ladder. When you get to the bottom there'll be a little chain hanging from the ceiling opposite the ladder. Pull it and the light will come on. Okay?"

"Okay," I said.

"There'll be shelves on your left. On one of the bottom two shelves there should be garbage bags. Grab one. There should be a box of vinyl gloves too. Throw that in the bag. Then check out the higher shelves. If there's a bottle of bleach up there, take that too. Got it?"

"What is this for?"

"It doesn't matter. Just do it. Garbage bag, gloves, bleach. Okay?"

"Okay."

"Good. Then turn and walk toward the light, through the narrow hallway. When you get to the next room there should be another little chain. Pull it. Then turn to your right. There will be a tarp hanging on the wall. Take it down, fold it up, put it in the bag. You'll see a number of bungee cords on the wall behind the tarp—throw those in the bag as well. Maybe you'll need two bags, actually. And then on the other side of the room, there's a bunk. Underneath the bunk you'll see two Rubbermaid tubs. One of them is filled with towels, if you could grab a few of those. Two or three towels. And that's it. Bring the bags back up here. Can you do that for me?"

"Yes," I said.

"Do you need me to repeat the list?"

"Garbage bags, on the shelves. Bleach. Gloves. And then in the next room, the tarp. Bungee cords. Two or three towels."

"Very good," Isaac said. He pointed his gun at Patti. "Go on then. Let's hurry."

I lowered myself down the ladder. The air grew a little cooler as I neared the bottom of the hole. I was actually in Leonard's secret lair. But as curious as I was to explore the bunker and see what my husband had been up to, there were more pressing concerns. Isaac. He had a gun. He'd done something with Dougie, and now he wanted bungee cords and bleach. He was a psychopath. He'd killed Leonard, I thought. He must have. Now he would kill me, and Patti. But no—I couldn't let him hurt Patti. Maybe there was something I could do to help her. Or maybe I'd bring him the things he wanted and he'd leave us alone.

When I reached the bottom of the ladder, I could see the general shape of the room by the band of sunlight coming in from above. I reached in front of me and felt around until I found the chain. I pulled it and the room lit up. There were the storage shelves, the water bottles, the soda, the canned food. It was strange, actually standing there after studying the room in Leonard's video for so long. I bent down and checked the bottom shelf, found the box of garbage bags. I pulled two from the box, then found the vinyl gloves. All kinds of cleaning products on the top shelf, but I didn't see any bleach.

"Hey," I called up the ladder, "I can't find the bleach."

"Just get the rest of the stuff," Isaac called down. "Hurry up."

I turned and stepped through the narrow hallway. I had to duck. I switched on the light when I reached the end and found myself in the second room. There was the bunk on my left. No shower curtain had been installed after all. Two tied-up garbage bags and a folded bedsheet lay atop the thin mattress. Mother's bedsheet, from the video. Opposite the hallway, a ladder reached up into a hole in the ceiling. To my right was the tarp, hanging from a beam. I pulled it down.

The gun rack from the video was now empty, but other supplies hung from pegs. An axe, ropes, some sort of tactical vest. I grabbed the bungee cords and stuffed them in the bag. Then the towels, from under the bunk. I had everything. I reached for the chain to turn off the light, then paused. On a wooden beam above the entrance to the hallway something had been written in black Sharpie.

THE NATURAL LIGHT OF GOD IS DEATH.

Those were Father Woodbine's words. They were carved into the bathroom door on The Farm. And now they were here, in Leonard's bunker. Written in Leonard's handwriting, it looked like. I remembered the video footage: Leonard had addressed someone specific. He was bringing them to his bunker. They lived or had lived in South West Detention Centre. And Leonard had the prison map. Where was Father Woodbine serving his sentence? I purposely avoided news of him and anything else to do with the Citizens of Light. Was he out now?

"What's going on?" Isaac's high-pitched voice shot down into the bunker.

"I'm coming," I shouted in return. I hurried back down the narrow hall. The bags weren't all that heavy, but it was awkward carrying them up the ladder. I managed, however. I passed them up to Isaac and he set them down.

"Right," he said. "That's swell. Now, back down the ladder. You too, Patti. Down you go."

"What about Dougie?" Patti said.

"Move it," Isaac said. "Now."

I climbed back down to the bottom and watched Patti descend. When she reached the halfway point, the hatch shut. There was a sliding sound, followed by a click.

"Patti," I said. "Go back up and try the door."

"But he said—"

"Just do it."

Patti climbed up and pushed against the door.

"It won't budge," she said. "What the fuck is going on?"

"We're locked in," I said.

29

I climbed up the ladder and tried the door myself, just to be sure. We were sealed in tight. The fact that the bunker could be locked from the outside was unsettling. I pounded on the door and screamed, but I knew it would have no effect. Nobody would hear me. And even if some hiker did happen by, they wouldn't notice the knocking or my voice. They'd hear a fly tapping on an acorn, the wind. I continued to scream anyway. My throat stung. I knocked until my hands were weak and sore, and eventually climbed back down. Patti was hugging her knees on the ground beside the shelves.

"Are you alright?"

She didn't answer. She had her face buried in her arms.

"Patti, hey. What are you doing?"

She looked up at me. She'd been crying. Her eyes looked huge and frightened in the glow of the naked bulb overhead.

"Did he kill Dougie?" Patti said.

"No, of course not. Isaac said he was fine."

"Dougie's dead."

"No. Come on. He's fine, Patti. Trust me. You don't really think that, do you?"

"We're going to die too."

"We'll get out of here soon. And then we'll go find Dougie straight away and you'll see that he's fine. Everything's okay."

Patti didn't say anything. I leaned down to put my hand on her shoulder but then changed my mind. I stood there with my arms at my sides.

"Dougie's fine," I said. "We're gonna be fine."

I remembered the axe. I stepped through the little hallway into the other room with the bunk and removed it from the wall. I hurried back to the ladder and climbed up to the hatch door. I had to lean back against the dirt wall, pushing against the ladder with my feet. There wasn't any room in the narrow tunnel to take a swing, but I could bash the axe upward. The top corner of the axe blade might splinter the wood, I hoped.

I thrusted the axe upward. No effect, it seemed. The door was solid.

I bashed it with the axe again. And again. My hands hurt, my arms were tired. I kept bashing the door. I hit it again and again, without results. The wood would have some tiny notches and superficial cracks, but I wouldn't break through. The door would remain shut until Isaac returned. Maybe I could wait up here, I thought, and get him with the axe when the hatch opened. If he returned. I kept hitting the door. I knew it was pointless, but I kept bashing away. I eventually became so fatigued I almost dropped the axe. It would've landed on Patti's head. I climbed back down. Blood trickled from my knuckles. I sat down on the ground next to Patti.

Hours passed. The small lightbulb attached to the wall above us began to dim. I wondered if Isaac would ever come back. Maybe he'd left us down there to die. Mother would wonder what had happened to me for the rest of her life. A citizen of some future society would discover our skeletons. But that type of thinking wouldn't help us get out. He'd come back. And I'd be ready.

I realized I was incredibly thirsty. Running through the muggy forest, plus all the screaming and axe-wielding. Patti was probably dehydrated, too. I stood up and found a case of water bottles on the shelf.

"Here," I said, handing a bottle to Patti. "Drink this."

She didn't react. I tucked the bottle in the crook of her elbow.

I took a long swig, then had a coughing fit. When this subsided, I finished off the bottle. I felt a little better. Less fuzzy.

"Come on," I said. "Let's see what else is down here. Maybe there's something we can use to get out. Or call for help."

Patti didn't move.

I picked up the axe and went back through the little hallway. I returned the axe to its place on the wall. The bulb in this room was significantly dimmer now, too. In the video, Leonard had mentioned a generator. In the corner of the room, beside the bunk, a ladder led up into the ceiling. I climbed into the darkness.

I reached up and searched with my hands for a light switch. I touched something wet and screamed. But I kept searching. My hand brushed past a small chain. I pulled on it and a light came on.

The room I entered was small and cramped. The ceiling sloped down on an angle, following the incline of the hill. There wasn't enough room to stand up, even at the ceiling's highest point by the ladder. The wet thing I'd touched was a garbage bag slick with condensation. There were more shelves next to the wall. More sealed buckets. More garbage bags. A short hallway—a tunnel you'd have to crawl through, actually—which led to another room. I got on my hands and knees.

This last room was more of a nook. There would've been space for me to squeeze inside if it was empty, but it wasn't. What had to be the generator sat in the middle of the floor. It was smaller than I'd thought—about the size of Isaac's air conditioner. The quiet hum the generator emitted was unexpected. I thought it would rumble like a car engine. A small screen indicated that the battery power was running low. If I wanted the lights to stay on, I'd need to change the battery, or charge it somehow. Maybe there were replacement batteries somewhere. I crawled backward out of the nook and into the other room.

I opened one of the buckets next to the wall. Oats. Another bucket filled with brown rice. An air purifier sat atop a box of spare air filters. Six tubs of Thirty-Day Emergency Food Storage Supply—some sort of freeze-dried meal rations. I checked the shelves. Canned beans and soups and spaghetti. A small space heater still in its package. A cereal box filled with candy bars. A bag filled with extension cords. A bag filled with boxes of LED lightbulbs. A tarp was covering something on the top shelf—I pulled it off.

A long black case lay underneath. Like some kind of wind instrument. I removed the case from the shelf and opened it up. A shotgun nestled in a purple beach towel.

Isaac eventually returned to the bunker. I'd fallen asleep sitting up against the wall by the ladder, next to Patti. The shotgun between my legs. I'd kept it wrapped up in the towel. I didn't want to alarm Patti, and I didn't want Isaac to know I'd found it right away. I woke up to the sound of the metal latch sliding out of place. We'd been sitting in darkness—the generator's battery had died, it seemed. Light spilled in from above as the door creaked open. Isaac's shadowy face appeared in the square opening. I wasn't sure if he could see me or not. He started climbing down the ladder. He shut the hatch door as he descended and the room went dark.

I stood up, dropped the towel. Readied the shotgun.

A blinding light washed over the room—Isaac had turned on a flashlight and was pointing it right into my eyes, only a few feet away. I squinted but didn't lower the gun. Patti hadn't moved. Isaac focused the light on my gun. His face looked calm. Expressionless, actually.

"It's not loaded," he said. "But you could bash my head in with the stock."

I wasn't sure what to do. I kept the gun aimed at his chest.

"Here," Isaac said. He reached out and put a hand on the barrel of the shotgun. He pulled at it gently, and I let go. He set it down against the wall.

"It's alright," Isaac said. "Maybe you'll get a chance later. Now let's go on into the other room."

I had to lift Patti up by her arms and practically push her into the next room. She must have been in a state of shock. She reminded me of one of those confused grandmothers you hear about, that wander into traffic. Isaac instructed us to sit down on the bunk.

He set his flashlight on a shelf in the corner, lighting the room. He removed his backpack and zipped it open. Pulled out a long, heavy-looking chain. A feeling of dread sank into my stomach. Isaac looped the chain around the wooden beam above the entrance—the one with Father Woodbine's words written on it. THE NATURAL LIGHT OF GOD IS DEATH. Isaac pulled and adjusted the chain until the two ends were of equal length.

"What are you doing?" I asked.

Isaac didn't say anything. There were shackles, or cuffs attached to the ends of the chain. He grabbed Patti's leg, attached one of the cuffs to her ankle. She didn't react. Then he reached for my leg.

"No!" I kicked at his hands.

Isaac stood up. He turned around and reached for the axe hanging on the wall.

"Hey," I said. "Please don't. I'll stop."

Isaac swung the axe back and then drove it into the wall above my head. I screamed. Patti screamed too. She jumped down onto the floor. Dirt poured down my back. Isaac set the axe down by his feet.

"I'm not fooling around here," he said. "You will behave

yourselves. That's just how it's got to be."

He knelt down and fastened the other cuff to my ankle. Patti and I were now tethered to each other. Attached to the beam.

Isaac picked up the axe again and walked over to the ladder, which led to the little room with the slanted ceiling. He took his flashlight and climbed up. I could hear him rummaging around.

"Patti," I whispered. "What do we do?"

She was crying, softly. She didn't respond.

"Oh God," I said.

The lights flickered back on. More shuffling sounds from above. The cuff was tight around my ankle—I tried adjusting it, but it wouldn't move. The metal dug into my skin. Eventually, Isaac climbed back down to us. A garbage bag in his hands. He'd left the axe up in the other room.

He removed several bottles of water from the bag and set them down on the ground in front of us. Then a loaf of bread and a jar of peanut butter. A package of plastic utensils. A roll of toilet paper. Then a thick book: *500 Sports Jokes*. He folded up the garbage bag, now empty, and walked back to the entryway. More sounds of shuffling around. He returned with a large plastic bucket. A bag of kitty litter was inside. He placed the bucket on the ground next to the other items.

"I'm sure you can guess what this is for," Isaac said. "I need to duck out again for a while. A few things to take care of. This should tide you over until I return."

"What are you going to do with us?" I asked.

"We'll see," Isaac said. "Hold tight."

30

With Patti and me each having an equal amount of chain, I could move in a radius of about four feet from the beam. I could increase that radius if Patti were to move closer to the beam and let me pull some of her chain over to my side. Regardless, there wouldn't be enough slack to reach any of the other areas—we were stuck in the little room with the bunk.

I asked Patti to step toward the beam and then moved closer to it myself, so there was some slack in the chain. I grabbed each side of the chain and started pulling at it, one side and then the other, so the chain would rub into the beam. I was hoping that it would create a groove in the wood and, eventually, with enough time and strength, I could cut right through. And then find some way to open the hatch door. But the chain kept slipping on the beam. The wood was strong. It would never work. And even if it did work, the ceiling might collapse. We'd be buried alive. I dropped the chain. I tried smashing the corner of the bathroom bucket down on the chain, but nothing happened. We were stuck. I sat down and rubbed my sore, red ankle where it chafed from the cuff.

Patti still wasn't talking, but I managed to get her to drink some water. I made us peanut butter sandwiches, but she wouldn't touch hers. I ate it. I flipped through the joke book. The jokes weren't so good.

Q: What kind of stories do basketball players tell?

A: Tall tales.

I started covering up the punchlines with my hand and trying to guess them, based on the set-ups. Why didn't the dog want to play football? Because whenever his teammates threw the ball, he would fetch it and bring it back to them, and they'd lose the point, I thought. But it was too long for the punchline. Maybe because the dog punctured the football with his teeth. The real answer was because it was a boxer. I wasn't sure if I understood the joke or not. A lot of the jokes were like that. Reading them made me angry.

Hours passed. I couldn't tell how many, though, or if it was night or day. I'd fallen into uneasy sleep a few times. Abstract, troubling dreams that bled through into my waking state. Patti lay on the bunk, while I stretched out on the floor. It was cold. The generator had shut off again and we sat in complete darkness. Like Moon Camp. This made it a little easier when I couldn't hold out any longer and had to urinate into the bucket. I was still shy about going to the bathroom in such a crude way, out in the open next to Patti, but there was nothing I could do. I crouched over the bucket and hummed to mask the sound. Afterward, I tried nudging the bucket into the hallway with my foot and I knocked it over. I scattered some kitty litter in the darkness, but the room still smelled like my pee.

Patti finally spoke. She said she was scared and that she wanted to leave. I said I was scared too, but that we would leave soon.

"What is this place?" Patti said. "I don't understand. Did Leonard live down here?"

"I think it's a criminal hideout," I said, though I wasn't so sure. Something strange was going on. The inscription on the beam. I hadn't told Patti about the Citizens of Light, or that a quote from my former cult leader was scrawled above our heads. Speaking it aloud would make it real. It *couldn't* be real. Maybe it was just a coincidence. "For the Mafia. Leonard owed them money and they must have ordered him to build it for them. In lieu of payment."

"Isaac doesn't seem like a mob guy. More like a serial killer."

"He's not a serial killer."

"And this is his torture chamber. Where he cuts his victims up."

"Patti, no."

Isaac eventually returned. I heard the door unlatch and watched light stream into the black, briefly, before he shut it again. Isaac turned on his flashlight and moved toward us. His silhouette appeared in the doorway.

"Sorry I took so long," he said. "How are you two getting along down here?"

Patti began to sob. She'd been crying, on and off, for hours now.

"Let us out of here," I said.

"I can't do that," Isaac said. "I'm sorry. But don't you fret. Everything is going to work out. It's interesting, actually. The universe putting us all together like this. This situation isn't what any of us planned on, but it might be exactly what we all need. It's kind of perfect."

"Please," I said. "You have to let us go. People know where we are and what we're doing. The police are going to come looking for us soon."

"I'm not going to hurt you. You don't need to worry. Trust me. Heck, you'll soon realize that we're all right where we need to be. I sure am sorry about the chain and everything, but all that's temporary. We'll sort things out soon and you'll be much more comfortable. You'll see."

Patti was shaking beside me. Her whole body quivered. I put my hands on her shoulders.

"You need to let us out of here," I said.

"You'll see," Isaac said. "This is exciting. Don't you worry."

Isaac sat in the little hallway that connected our room to the entrance. He wore the same plaid shirt and black jeans he wore when he first locked us in the bunker. With his back to the wall, he pulled a piece of paper out of his pocket and stared at it. He kept glancing over at me to see if I was watching. Then he'd look back at the paper and sort of laugh through his nose and smile.

After a few minutes of this, he came over to me and showed me the piece of paper. It was a photograph of Jess, the server from Roswell's. She was leaning up against a car and smiling.

"That's my girl," Isaac said.

"Okay," I said.

"Maybe you saw her at the restaurant. She's really something else. You'll get to meet her."

He moved back over to the hallway and sat looking at the picture for a while longer. Then he left. Several hours later he returned with a crazed look on his face. He seemed furious, breathing heavily through his nose. There were bandages wrapped around his hand.

"For Pete's sake," Isaac said. "It smells like dogshit in here. I can't breathe."

He rummaged around the shelves by the entrance, then started marching between the two rooms, his fingers pressing down on the trigger of a spray bottle. Lemon air freshener. The bunker smelled like chemicals for hours after he left. I had to pull my shirt collar up over my nose.

"Can I say something terrible?" Patti lay on the bunk, looking up at the ceiling. I was on the ground reading through the joke book again.

"What do you mean?"

"Obviously, I'm heartbroken that Dougie is dead. That he was murdered."

"Patti, come on. You don't know that."

"If I'm being honest, though, I'm also kind of relieved that he's gone. That I don't have to worry about Dougie anymore, if we somehow get out of here. We *can't* get back together. I don't have to have his dinner ready. Or hear him complain about everything I do. The fights. Isn't that terrible?"

"Well, no. I'm sure it's complicated."

"And this is just a small part of me that feels relieved. Most of me feels unbelievably sad. It's just that there's a tiny piece that is so happy I don't have to see Dougie anymore. Plus, I'm allowed to say this because I'm going to get murdered too."

"Nobody's getting murdered. Come on."

"Did you feel at all relieved when Leonard died? I know it's different."

"Patti, no."

"Do you think I'm terrible? Dougie didn't deserve this, obviously. And it's my fault he came here, too. If I had just gone home with him. Maybe he was right about me."

"What do you mean?"

"Maybe I ruined his life."

"What? He abused you."

"I don't know." Patti burst into tears. I put my arms around her and she buried her head in my chest, sobbing.

"It's okay," I said. "It's not your fault, Patti."

Things went on like this for days, or what felt like days. It was impossible to keep track of time. Isaac would leave for hours and then return to empty our bathroom bucket and make sure we had enough water and peanut butter. Sometimes he'd sit and talk with me, and sometimes he would move around the bunker wordlessly, doing what needed to be done and then leaving. Sometimes his demeanour was friendly, and sometimes he'd be cold and almost threatening. It was impossible to predict which version of Isaac would come down the ladder to us.

One day, while he was in one of his more pleasant moods, I asked Isaac about Leonard. How he'd ended up out here, and what the bunker was for. Isaac sat cross-legged on the floor next to the bucket. I was leaning up against the bunk, where Patti lay sleeping, or pretending to sleep.

"I'm sure you recognized that," Isaac said, pointing to the wooden beam above us. The quote from Father Woodbine.

"The Citizens of Light," I said. I wondered if Patti was listening. She would have no idea what we were talking about.

"'The natural light of God is death,'" Isaac said. "Do you understand what that means?"

"It means that Father Woodbine was insane."

"Come on. Seriously."

"It means that death and pain and chaos are not bad things," I said, a slight mocking tone in my voice. I hadn't thought about this stuff in decades. I was surprised to find Woodbine's teachings still intact inside my brain. I guess they'll be lodged inside there forever. "That we use hierarchies to make sense of the world and order things in our minds, but that nothing in nature is better than or less than anything else in the eye of the God-Spirit. Stepping on a rusty nail is essentially the same as, like, eating birthday cake."

"Yes!" Isaac said. He clapped his hands. "That's part of it. That's just swell. You remember."

"But that's crazy. If you believed that, you'd have no problem stepping on a rusty nail right now."

"No," Isaac said. "You've got it all wrong. I understand on a theoretical level that pain is the same as not-pain. But I can't truly commit to the idea and inflict pain on myself with indifference. Just like how I can't kill myself, even though I know it doesn't matter if I do. Intellectually. I still have 'binary thinking.' The false hierarchies that order the universe are hardwired into my brain. It's part of The Great Distortion."

"But what's the point then, if it's all theoretical?"

"To live a more truthful existence. To live in the real world as much as possible. Not some phoney-baloney hologram. To die a real death, too. Close to Ka-Ni. And the more you understand about the nature of reality, the more authentic your experience of living and dying will become. It's something to strive for."

"But if there's no hierarchy and nothing is better than anything else, then who cares if your experience is more authentic? How can it be better to live more truthfully if you don't believe in 'better?'"

"You're right, authenticity is not better. It's just more authentic. I'm not placing a value on living in the real world. I'm just saying that the real world is more real. More in tune with the God-Spirit."

"That doesn't make any sense."

"You just don't understand. You've lost your way. But it will come back to you."

"What does any of this have to do with Leonard?"

"Your late husband understood Woodbine's vision," Isaac said. "He was helping me revive the movement."

"You're full of shit."

"It's the truth. Leonard built this place. For Father Woodbine. A place for him to lie low once we got him out of prison."

"Out of South West Detention Centre."

"That's right. Once everything falls into place and we finally free him, Woodbine will come here and then, eventually, we'll take him to the new farm. We've already purchased the property. You're going to help me set up everything there. You and Patti."

"You can't be serious. Leonard wouldn't be a part of this madness."

"It's not madness. Far from it. And I think you know that."

"How did you even meet Leonard?"

Isaac described how, a few years earlier, he'd read about the Citizens of Light in a magazine article and was instantly fascinated by Woodbine's ideas. Isaac had for a long time been disturbed by the way people walked around with their heads in the clouds, oblivious to what was really going on. Death was inevitable, and this was a big deal, he felt, but everyone lived as if it wasn't. It was absurd. Woodbine seemed to understand this, too. Isaac read everything he could about the cult, combing through what he felt were sensationalized and unbalanced reports for scraps of Woodbine's philosophical teachings. He tracked down news footage and watched it all on a loop. The more he learned, the more it resonated with him. It turned into an obsession. He reached out to Woodbine himself, and eventually was able to set up phone calls and visits. He became a student of the prisoner. And then, Isaac said, he began to track down the former members of the Citizens of Light. He and Woodbine were going to rebuild.

"Which led me to you," Isaac said.

"What do you mean?"

"I came to Toronto. Parked down the street from your house. I watched you and Leonard and your mother."

"No."

"One evening, you were off at work. Your mother was asleep. Leonard had gone out somewhere and I guess I missed him coming back home. I wanted to try and get inside. See if you kept anything from your time with Woodbine. But also just to see how you lived. Look through your computer. A diary would have been real swell. I wanted to get a sense of whether you might one day join Woodbine and me in resurrecting the movement. I went into the backyard and Leonard saw me peering through your bedroom window. He ran out and caught up with me at my car. I couldn't get my keys in the door in time. He threw me down and I clonked my head on the pavement. Blood everywhere. Good old Leonard took me to the hospital himself."

"You're lying," I said. "Leonard never told me about this."

"That's because I told him not to."

"Why would he listen to you?"

"I came to on the way to the hospital. We started talking. I was completely honest with him. I explained how I was researching Woodbine's movement and wanted to see how all the former members were doing. We started talking about the Citizens of Light. He was mad as all heck, and assumed I was crazy. But he still listened. By the time we left the emergency room, I'd planted a seed in your husband. He could see there was something there. And I recognized the light in Leonard's eyes. I knew he would understand. I asked for his email address. We began a correspondence."

"No," I said.

"I'm sorry," Isaac said. "But, yes."

31

Isaac left us a Ziploc bag full of moist towelettes so we could clean ourselves. A deodorant stick for us to share. We still smelled terrible. We didn't have a change of clothes. Isaac replaced the joke book with a thick document he had printed out himself. He'd taken notes during his visits and calls with Father Woodbine and typed them up for us to read. Most of it was incomprehensible. Manic ramblings about society and our fractured relationship with the God-Spirit Ka-Ni. Long, convoluted descriptions of dreams Woodbine had in prison. Crude diagrams of new farm facilities Isaac had drawn based on Woodbine's descriptions. One diagram was labelled SCREAM CLOSETS.

Memories of The Farm surfaced. Smells, the faces of other recruits. Woodbine's face. I remembered the time when Woodbine brought everyone from Moon Camp up into the den. It was the middle of the night. He opened up two fresh sets of kitchen knives and passed them around. He instructed us to hold the knives to our throats. He held a knife to his own throat too. He had this wild, possessed look. We chanted "Do it! Do it!" in unison. Over and over. After twenty minutes, he gathered up the knives and sent us back down to the basement. Lying in my bunk afterward, I couldn't tell if I was alive or dead.

Isaac brought a fat brown envelope down from the upper room and set it in front of me.

"I just found this," he said. "Tucked behind Leonard's sleeping bag."

I opened the envelope. It was filled with dog-eared scripts. My scripts. Mostly *Riders of Exley* episodes I'd written, but there was also a *Hot in Cleveland* spec in there and two versions of a *Frasier* spec, in case they ever decided to reboot the series. Leonard must have printed them off and brought them down into his secret bunker to read.

I started crying. Isaac left. Patti reached over and grabbed my hand.

"You never told me you were in that cult," Patti leaned against the wall, scooping peanut butter from the jar with her finger. I opened my eyes. I'd drifted off on the bunk.

"I don't like to talk about it."

"I remember hearing about it on the news. That's messed up you were there. Why did you join?"

"I don't know. I was young. Mother and I had a big fight. The guy who told me about it was so nice, and everyone there was so welcoming. I didn't know what I was really getting into."

"I've watched a lot of docs about cults. Apparently, they prey on people with Schizotypal thinking. Do you have Schizotypal thinking?"

"I'm not sure."

"Yeah, I don't really know what it means. I bet I would join a cult. It would take two seconds for them to recruit me. Cults are so fascinating."

"I didn't know I was in a cult. I don't think I even knew what cults were, at the time. I just thought everyone there was so great. Back home, Mother was always high-strung and temperamental. My dad had left us, and then he died. None of my friends understood what it was like. I remember being angry all of the time. But then I got to The Farm and people listened to me. They didn't see me as a problem, or an obstacle. They seemed to actually care about me."

"What about all the death stuff that you and Isaac were talking about? Did you believe all that?"

"It made sense to me at the time. These were the people that made me feel good about myself. I kind of just went along with whatever they said. I trusted them."

"What about after you left? And the leader was arrested and everything?"

"I don't know. The whole thing felt like it was a dream, afterward. Like none of it was real. It made me feel sick to my stomach, thinking about it. So, I tried not to think about it."

"I'm sorry, Colleen. Jesus. I had no idea."

"I'd found people that made me feel good about myself, I thought. But it was all fake. So I decided that I was right all along: I didn't have any worth. I was a problem. Since then, I've tried to just keep to myself and stay out of everyone's way. Then I finally opened myself up to Leonard, and that turned out to be fake too. He had this whole secret life."

"That wasn't fake. He still loved you. People care about you. Your mother cares."

"I know, she does."

"I hate pretty much everyone. The world is filled with idiots and creeps. But you, I actually don't mind."

"You don't?"

A few hours later, Isaac came back down the ladder and handed us cleaning supplies. We had to disinfect everything in the room, including our own chains. Isaac sat in the corner and stared. He didn't say a word. When we finished, he stood up and inspected the room, slowly. He grunted a few times, but still said nothing. And then he left.

He came back later in a more talkative mood. He brought us Snickers bars and stood stooped over in the little doorway. He tried asking Patti about her life, but she would only give terse, one-word answers. He showed her the photo of Jess the server that he'd shown me.

"She's going to live on the new property with us," Isaac said. "She's my girl."

Patti didn't react. Isaac focused back in on me. He showed me the photo of Jess again. I said she looked pretty. We returned to the subject of Isaac's relationship with Leonard. Patti was sleeping now. I asked Isaac to tell me more about how he became involved with my husband.

According to Isaac, he'd emailed Leonard an apology the day after their emergency room visit, along with a link to an article about Father Woodbine. Leonard waited a week to reply, but he did reply. He said he appreciated the apology and that the article was interesting, but Woodbine was still a monster. Isaac had him on the hook. He sent another article. They discussed it and continued writing back and forth. Isaac hadn't had any luck tracking down the other former cult members, and so he decided to focus his efforts entirely on me and my husband. He sent Leonard long emails, asking for his opinion on different aspects of Woodbine's teachings. Made Leonard feel like his ideas had value. Sometimes the emails would stray from the Citizens of Light and venture into personal matters. Isaac wanted to know more about his new friend, and so he wove revealing, intimate details from his own life into the discussion. His strained relationship with his father, his inability to maintain any kind of social life as an adult. In response, Leonard hinted at his past struggles with addiction. Isaac lied and said that he was in recovery, too. Then Isaac would relate all of this back to Woodbine's ideas: "Addiction is a form of death-denial; let go of your fear of death, and you will no longer seek comfort from the bottle or the needle." Slowly, Leonard began to share Isaac's obsession with Woodbine. The ideas started to click. Isaac wanted to lend him a book. Leonard turned this offer down, but eventually accepted. Obviously, he never told me about any of this. The two men met up at a diner in Hamilton.

"Things progressed from there," Isaac told me. "We'd meet every week. Sometimes twice a week. Or we'd talk on the phone. Leonard transitioned from curious student to dedicated activist, working alongside me to bring Woodbine's vision to life. It was really something. When things got more serious and we started work on the bunker, Leonard became worried about the risk involved with conventional methods of communication. Phone calls and emails leave a trail, he said."

"You used *Reindeer Island*," I said.

"That's right."

"You're Bonsai. I knew it. You left me those messages. How did you know I was in Niagara Falls?"

"The head of Fallsview security you spoke to is on my father's payroll. You were asking questions about me and the Russian that got caught. My father's guys thought you were some nosy journalist or investigator, poking around in our business. They had you followed, to see what you were up to. But I had a feeling it must be you. I didn't want you poking around either, so I left the messages. I thought it would scare you off."

"You knew our room number at the hotel."

"Yeah, well, I know people. When my contact at the Hilton didn't find your name on file, I thought you might have checked in under a fake name. But then I called around and found you at the Queen Fallsview. The whole thing took five minutes."

"My God. I always wondered who Bonsai was when I started playing. You always ran away. You knew it was me the whole time?"

"I figured it had to be. I probably should have stopped playing, but it was strange. Whenever I saw Heartsong running around in the game, it felt like Leonard was still alive, controlling him."

"So you and Leonard really used *Reindeer Island* to communicate?"

"It was Leonard's idea. I thought it was a touch silly at first. Paranoid. Nobody was paying any attention to our phone calls or emails. I realized later he wasn't so concerned that the RCMP would discover our conversations. He didn't want *you* to find out what was going on. So I went along with it. I downloaded *Reindeer Island*. I didn't want to discourage him."

"But how did you use it? You can't talk or type anything."

"You can, actually. You know the chapel?"

"Sure."

"Inside, there's a big screen up on the wall. Like one of those scrolling news tickers. If you stand in front of it, you can type messages into it for other players to see. You just have to switch on the power in the basement. We were able to plan meet-ups this way, without leaving any record of our conversation. Leonard kept me updated on his progress with the bunker. It felt ridiculous at times, but it was also kind of fun. And Leonard's worries were eased."

"I thought my husband was playing an innocent computer game," I said. "He was plotting with you the whole time."

"Well, not always," Isaac said. "Mostly we'd just enjoy the game. We spent hours unlocking the island's secret together. I'd never really been interested in video games, but I had a swell time with this one. With Leonard. I miss playing with him."

"Then you shouldn't have killed him."

"I didn't."

According to Isaac, a week of living in the bunker had passed by this point, which seemed about right. Patti and I were both weak, not sleeping well, not eating properly. At turns delirious, bored, or crushed by the bleakness of the situation. But there were moments of clarity, and in one of these moments we came up with a plan to free ourselves.

Which each visit, Isaac spent more and more time preaching to us about the God-Spirit Ka-Ni and Woodbine's philosophy of inviting death inside of your heart. I wasn't sure if Father Woodbine was directing him from prison, or if he was acting on his own accord, but it was apparent that Isaac was trying to turn me back into a devout follower and bring Patti into the fold for the first time. Every day he'd order us to scrub and disinfect everything within our reach so that our area was spotless. While we cleaned, Isaac would sit in the corner and deliver little improvised sermons. Some of it I remembered from my time on The Farm, and some of it was new. All of it was crazy. Woodbine's skill was in taking some uncontroversial, widely accepted idea—like that death is something we all have to contend with, or that the contrast of evil in the world allows for the existence of goodness—and then using vague, convoluted language to suggest that these ideas inevitably lead to more controversial and absurd conclusions. Like that sleeping in a graveyard and touching corpses will bring you closer to understanding the universe. Isaac adopted the same technique but wasn't as convincing as Woodbine had been. I wondered how long that would last. Maybe Isaac would eventually brainwash us into becoming followers. The more time we spent locked up in the bunker, the less resistant we would become.

I asked Patti if she thought he would brainwash us, and she said it wasn't likely. Then her eyes lit up. She had an idea: What if we played along with Isaac's ramblings, and pretended that we were convinced by his efforts to indoctrinate us? Maybe he would eventually trust us and let his guard down. It seemed far-fetched and like it might take a while to set in motion though. If he didn't see through our plan right away, it could take weeks or months for him to leave us an opening to escape. We needed out of there as soon as possible.

It might seem more convincing, we realized, if only one of us pretended to fall under Isaac's spell. It could speed things along, too. I alone would act as if Woodbine's ideas were getting through to me, again. Patti would pretend she was horrified by this. We would turn against each other, and so Isaac would begin to trust me. Maybe he'd present me with an opportunity to betray him and attempt an escape, and I wouldn't take it. Let him think I was acting out of loyalty. Really, I'd wait for him to truly lower his guard. And then when the next opening arrived, I would make a move.

Isaac returned to the bunker in a foul mood. He scolded us for the state of the room and our odour. He barked at us to start cleaning and sat in the corner, watching us silently. No sermons this time. Patti started crying while wiping down a shelf and Isaac threw his flashlight at the wall. I decided not to start in on the plan this visit.

Isaac left and didn't return for what felt like days. We'd gone through our loaf of bread and were down to the bottom of the peanut butter jar. Three bottles of water left. If Isaac were to get into an accident, or if he was sent off to prison for something and didn't tell anyone where we were, we would die. Or maybe Isaac would intentionally abandon us. Leave us to rot.

"Does this feel the same as when you were a teenager?" Patti had her head on my legs. We were both lying on the ground. I thought she was asleep and her voice startled me.

"What?"

"When you were living with the cult. Was it like this at all?"

"Well, no. I wasn't locked in against my will. I mean, not really."

"What do you think would have happened if the police hadn't shown up? If Woodbine never went to prison and all that."

"I don't know. I guess I would've stayed there."

"So, you were happy then. Maybe this won't be that bad. You liked being on The Farm."

"Sometimes, maybe. But I missed Mother. And a lot of it was really horrible."

"But you would have stayed. You were happier in the cult than you were at home."

"I don't think so. No, it was terrible."

"Then why did you stay?"

"Why did you stay with Dougie?"

Isaac returned in a more congenial mood. He emptied and cleaned our toilet bucket, then brought us down more water bottles, peanut butter, and a fresh loaf of bread.

"Sorry for the long absence," he said. "My father had me doing something and I couldn't get away until it was finished. But things are on track. It won't be much longer before I can bring you two out to the new property. Jess too. Maybe someone else—I'm working on it. The community is growing. You just need to hold tight."

"It's okay," I said. "We're fine."

"Really? That's good to hear. We need to get the bunker ready for Father Woodbine. I've been in contact with one of the guards at South West and things are looking pretty darn good there too. The guard's on my father's payroll and I think I can get him to help us out, which would be huge."

"That's wonderful," I said.

"Oh?" Isaac said. "You think that's wonderful?"

"Well, yes. I've had a lot of time to think down here, and it's made me realize that you're right. Maybe it is time to rebuild the Citizens of Light. Now that I'm older and I've had time to reflect, I can see the value in Father Woodbine's vision. It's coming back to me. I can feel a connection to the God-Spirit again."

"Really?" Isaac said. "What about you, Patti? Have you had any great realizations?"

Patti stared down at her feet.

"She'll come around," I said. "I'll help her see the way. This is all just new to her."

"Right," Isaac said. He stared at me, his face expressionless. I smiled back at him, but then had to look away. His eyes were like syringes.

"Don't worry about Patti," I said. "I'll talk to her."

Isaac didn't respond. I glanced up at him—his cold eyes were still fixed on me.

"She'll come around," I said.

"This is disappointing, Colleen," Isaac said.

"Excuse me?"

"Do you really think I'm so stupid? I won't tolerate dishonesty. Things were moving along so well. You will need to be punished."

"But—"

"Quiet."

Isaac walked over and picked up the bag of kitty litter. He placed it inside of the bathroom bucket.

"You will have to use the floor now, like dogs," he said. "I want you to think about what you've done. Things were going so well."

He took the bucket and left.

32

Not long after Isaac left, I had to relieve my bowels. I couldn't hold it any longer. It was diarrhea and it burned. I bawled my eyes out the whole time. I covered it up with a tarp afterward, but the smell was overpowering. I wanted to die in that moment. Patti tried to comfort me, but the horror of the situation had finally become overwhelming. I didn't feel human.

After an hour or so of crying and shaking, I began to calm down. I even slept a little. When I awoke, Patti got me to drink some water. The generator had died again. We sat in the darkness.

"If you could walk out of here right now, what would you do?" Patti said.

"What do you mean? I'd call the police."

"Okay, but after that."

"I don't know. Make sure Mother is okay."

"Yeah, but aside from all that. You walk out of here and see your mom and Isaac gets murdered in jail and everything is sorted. Then what?"

"I don't know. What would you do?"

"I'd have a long shower and brush my hair. I'd put on clean clothes—my sweats. I'd curl up on the couch and watch TV. I don't even care what show."

"Yeah?"

"Yeah. And make coffee. And order in from Tuscano's. And look at porn on my iPad."

"Oh."

"I guess I want to go back to Toronto. Back home. But I don't want Dougie to be there. I hope he's alive and okay, but I want him to be somewhere else. Like Europe. Do you think Isaac killed him?"

"Patti, no. Don't say that."

"We both heard the gunshots."

"That doesn't mean anything."

"Yeah, well."

When Isaac finally returned to the bunker, it felt like a decade had passed. Isaac said it was a day and a half. He changed the generator's batteries and brought us Clorox wipes, paper towels, and a fresh bag of litter. He went into the other room while Patti and I did our best to clean up our area. I almost threw up while dealing with the mess I'd left under the tarp, but I kept it together. Once we were finished, Isaac took away our trash.

"I hope you've used your time to think about what you've done," Isaac said. "I've been doing some thinking too. We need to get you two ready for the work ahead, up at the property. Which means you'll be adopting a new exercise regimen I've worked out. To get you two into proper shape. I'll be bringing you protein shakes from now on as well. Can't have you getting weak on me. I've got some other ideas too, but we don't need to get into that now. Anyway, here."

He handed us each a plastic bottle. The label said CORE POWER HIGH PROTEIN MILK SHAKE.

"We'll need to do something about that darn smell in here," Isaac continued. "Maybe set up some fans and leave the door open for a while. Which could be risky. I don't know. But this definitely won't do for our guest of honour. I should bring you some fresh clothes. Anyway, I'll show you the exercises. Both of you, stand up."

He had us perform squats, push-ups, lunges, and a few different stretches. It was awkward with the cramped space and chain connecting us, but Patti and I followed Isaac's directions as best as we could. We were both sore and weak and every movement was painful. But we did them and Isaac seemed satisfied.

"It'll get easier," Isaac said. "We'll go again tomorrow. You'll soon see results. This is good. Drink your shakes. I'm leaving again, but I won't be so long this time. I'm going to try and spend more time down here with you two. Get some real discussions going. Get you both on track. There'll be more structured lessons going forward. Things are ramping up. This is going to be incredible."

He left. The protein shake was hard to get down, but I felt a little better afterward. We'd been subsisting on just peanut butter for so long. I could almost feel the nutrients swimming around in my body.

"You don't really think I killed him, do you?"

I awoke to find Isaac sitting on the ground next to me. The lights were on. Sweat gathered on Isaac's forehead. His tiny eyes seemed to be pushing against the sockets, trying to escape.

"Sorry?"

"You need to know that I didn't kill Leonard," Isaac said. "I never did anything to hurt him. He was my friend."

"Why should I believe you?"

"Because it's the darn truth. Why would I lie? I have you here now. There's nothing you can do. If I had killed him, I'd say so."

"What about Dougie? Patti's husband."

He didn't say anything. I looked up at Patti—she was lying on the bunk behind me, her back turned. I couldn't tell if she was listening or not.

"See? You're full of shit."

"I didn't say anything," Isaac said. "But let's stay on topic. This is important. I need you to know that I didn't kill Leonard. He was my friend."

"So you say."

"He was. I don't see a lot of people. And all the guys who work for my father are jackasses. Each and every one. Spending time with these morons had this effect on me, where I thought everyone was like that. It felt like the whole world had gone crazy. That everybody was rude and condescending. Treating me like I'm some mental case. But Leonard wasn't like that. He was respectful. Kind. Open-minded. If it weren't for him and Jess, I'd have no hope for humanity. I know it doesn't compare with what you went through losing him, but I was devastated when I found out what happened to Leonard. Death means nothing to the deceased, but Leonard's death sure meant something to me. That's why I came to the funeral. I had to say goodbye to my friend."

"Some friend," I said. "He'd still be here if he hadn't met you."

"And sometimes I wish he hadn't. I think about that every day. You know that picture you saw of me in the paper? That's a picture of a broken man. I had given up on everything, even Woodbine. Nothing mattered. Leonard was gone. Jess wouldn't talk to me outside of her work. Or even at work, for the most part. The universe had failed me. Until you came looking for me. Leonard's death was a true test, and I don't think I could've passed it without you. I owe you a great deal of gratitude."

"What were you even doing at the casino?"

"A job for my father. You read about the Russian scam artist?"

"Yes."

"My father had been tipped off that he'd be coming. My dad got me the job at the casino so I could watch out for the Russian and bring him in. Before he took off with his winnings. Blackmail him. Get him to work for my father instead. But security got to him first. And not the security who worked for my dad. The cops were called. Some of the jackasses in my father's organization think I actually snitched."

"Okay, so let's say you didn't kill Leonard. What happened to him then?"

"You know what happened. He took his own life. I understand that that might be hard for you to believe, but it's the truth."

"But why? Because of Woodbine? All the 'death is the natural light of God' bullshit?"

"Father Woodbine never preached self-destruction. You know that. It's more complicated. Hard to get a definitive answer with something like this. There's always a combination of internal and external factors. But there's something you should know."

"What?"

"Before Leonard's passing, I'd been putting pressure on him. I wanted him to bring you out here. To the bunker."

"Why?"

"You were an original member. I knew it would please Father Woodbine. I thought it would be an important step for Leonard, too. He'd come such a long way and had accomplished so much, but he wasn't fully committed to the cause. By keeping his important work secret, he was living a double life. And the guilt of keeping all this hidden from you was crushing him. Think of the work he could have done if he lived just the one life, focused, in service of the Citizens of Light. Like me."

"And Leonard didn't want to bring me here."

"He did—or he said he did. He kept saying that he needed more time. That he needed to show you what we were doing in a way that wouldn't scare you off. He was sure that if he found the perfect way to tell you about it, you would happily join us without any coercion. But I wasn't so naïve. You wouldn't come willingly. I became fed up with Leonard putting things off. Fed up with his lack of commitment. I ordered him to bring you here."

"What did he say?"

"He said he would do it," Isaac said. I looked up at him. He had turned to face the entrance. "It was a Thursday evening. We were down here, testing the air-filtration system he'd bought. I told him that before the weekend was over, he needed to bring you in. I said if he didn't, he was out. If he couldn't prove his devotion to Father Woodbine and the cause, we would forge ahead without him. He begged me to reconsider, but I was firm. He agreed to do it. I left."

"What happened?"

Isaac didn't say anything. His back was still turned to me.

"Isaac."

"That was the last time I saw Leonard."

33

Isaac left us alone again. Patti had slept through everything Isaac said about my husband. I didn't fill her in. Instead I listened to her talk about the food she wanted to eat until she fell asleep again. In the silence that followed, I couldn't stop picturing Leonard. Down here, in the very same room. Frustrated, alone. Grabbing his father's hunting rifle from the wall. Climbing up the ladder, walking out into the woods. Deliberate, calculated. I needed to think about something else.

I started working on a new *Riders of Exley* script. Isaac hadn't left us any writing implements, so I had to just think of my episode and leave it at that. Mary Valentine wakes up in the middle of the night and creeps down to the stables. Opens all the gates, rouses the horses, ushers them out to the pasture, and leads them past the fence, into the parking lot. "Go on," she says. Mary then makes her way to the janitor's shed. Beside the lawnmower she finds a canister of gas. On a shelf, a box of long matches. She takes these items over to the dormitories and down into the basement. Walks up and down the hallways, leaving a trail of gasoline. Up the stairs, into the lobby. Strikes three matches at once and drops them into the pool of gas collected near her feet. Then she walks up the stairs to the second floor. Down the hall. She hears the fire alarm go off.

It's loud. She continues toward her room. Students are scrambling out of bed, into the hall. Panicking. Mary walks calmly past them all. Penelope, Mary's bunkmate, comes running out of their room with her parakeet in its cage. "Come on!" Penelope says, but Mary ignores her. Enters her room. Lies down on her bunk. Eyes closed, listening to the sounds of shrill voices and hurried footsteps echoing down the hall. The smell of smoke coming through the vents. Mary falls asleep, a smile on her face. Fade to black. Credits.

I had this dream where I was in my bed at home and a mouse was chewing on my pillow. The sound kept me awake. I told the mouse to go away, but it kept chewing. Really close to my ear. I was too tired to move my head. I awoke in the bunker and could still hear the chewing noise. I looked over at Patti. She was on her knees by the room entrance, digging at the ground. Using the cap from our deodorant stick.

"Hey," I said. "What are you doing?"

"Grab something and help me out here," Patti said. "We're making a trap."

"What do you mean?"

"We'll dig a hole, right here. Deep as we can manage. Cover it with the tarp, then spread some of the dirt on top so it looks normal. Next time Isaac walks in here, he'll step right into it. Maybe he'll break his leg. Either way, we'll surprise him. We can both hold him down and get the key for these chains."

"I don't know, Patti. How do we even know he has the key on him?"

"We don't. But fuck it, he probably does. You have a better idea?"

"How far along are you?"

Patti moved to the side so I could see her progress. There was a divot in the floor about the size of a dessert plate.

"This is only a few minutes of work," Patti said. "But it'll go faster if we're both digging. Find something. If you take the spray part off the empty Windex bottle you could use the opening. Isaac could come back any minute."

I grabbed the Windex and joined Patti by the entrance. The ground was pretty solid—it would take forever to dig a hole deep enough. But I kept at it. Dust soon filled the small room. We pulled our shirt collars up over our noses and squinted. My fingers were sore as hell. We didn't seem to be making any progress. The divot was maybe a little wider.

"Fuck!" Patti said.

She whipped the deodorant lid at the ground. It ricocheted under the bunk.

"I need the paper towel," Patti said. She held out her hand. Her knuckles were bleeding. I guess she'd slipped and scraped them on the ground.

I shuffled over to the bunk to fetch the paper towel roll. The cleaning supplies were in a box underneath.

"Grab my lid, too," Patti said. "I think it's under there some-where."

I couldn't see anything, so I reached underneath the bunk and felt around the area where I saw the lid slide. There were two Rubbermaid tubs. I couldn't find the deodorant lid though. Nothing in between the tubs, or up against the wall. It must have ended up all the way at the back. I went to pull the larger of the two tubs out from under the bunk, but it was a tight fit. I had to wrestle with it a bit. As I slid the tub out, something fell on the ground. I assumed it was the deodorant lid.

I reached under the bunk and pulled out an envelope. There was tape stuck to the top of it. It had been taped to the underside of the bunk.

"What's that?" Patti said.

I opened the envelope. It was filled with large bullets. Six of them. Shotgun shells.

"Holy shit," Patti said. "Are those bullets? I wonder what else is hidden around here."

"I think these are for the shotgun," I said.

"Too bad we can't just throw them really fast at Isaac."

"Oh my God."

"What?"

"It's still here," I said. "I think. The shotgun. Isaac left it in the other room by the ladder. I'm pretty sure it's still there."

"Seriously? Jesus. If only we could get it."

"Maybe we can."

I looked at the chain, the beam, the entrance to the room. If the chain was a few feet longer, I thought, we might be able to reach into the front room. And if the shotgun was still in there and positioned close enough, we could grab it.

"What if one of us climbs up there?" I said. "If you can get your ankle right up next to the beam, that might give me enough slack."

"Worth a try."

Patti stood up and reached over her head. She walked closer to the wall and gripped the beam with both hands. Then she climbed the wall with her feet until they were up next to the beam. She dug the sides of her feet into the beam, clinging to it like a sloth.

"Yes!" I said. "Can you do it facing the other way, with your feet closer to the hallway?"

"Shit." Patti's feet dropped. She let go of the beam and stood there, panting. "That's hard. I don't know how long I can hold on for. But yeah, I can probably do it the other way. Do you think this'll be enough? You'll have to be quick."

I dropped to my hands and knees in front of the little hallway, underneath the beam. Patti stood above me. The light was still on in the entrance room, but I couldn't see if the shotgun was there or not.

"Are you ready?" Patti said.

"Ready."

The chain rattled as she kicked her legs up. I looked up at her feet clinging to the beam above me.

"Go!" Patti said.

I crawled through as fast as I could. Only a few feet from the end of the hallway, I felt resistance. I stopped immediately, so that I didn't jerk the chain and pull Patti down from the beam. I carefully lay down flat on my belly and stretched out my arms—I was able to reach into the entrance room.

"Hurry," Patti's muffled voice sounded behind me.

I reached around frantically. I could see that the shotgun wasn't right in front of me—just part of the shelves, and part of the ladder. But there were blind spots around the corners of the entrance that were within reach. I felt an empty garbage bag. I threw it aside. A bucket. And then I touched something that felt right. Cold metal. The right shape, leaning up against the wall. I grabbed it and pulled it toward me—it was the shotgun.

I shuffled backward as fast as I could, dragging the heavy gun. Patti was screaming.

"I got it. I'm coming."

She landed on my back as I crawled through the entrance into our little room. Her knee in my spine—the pain was incredible. But it didn't matter. We had a way out.

Time stretched. It was torture, not knowing when Isaac would return to the bunker. Or if he even would. But he'd come back, I knew. It took us a while to figure out, but we successfully loaded two of the shells into the shotgun. We leaned it up against the wall next to the entrance, where Isaac wouldn't see. When Isaac came down the ladder, I would pick up the shotgun and ready it. When he stepped into our room, I'd have it pointed right at him. Patti would show him the extra bullets, so he'd know we'd found the ammo. Make him unlock the cuffs, then put them on *his* ankles. Lock *him* inside the bunker. Maybe we'd even wait a few days before telling the police, just to give him a taste of what we'd been through.

"If he tries anything, you have to shoot him," Patti said.

"I will," I said. "But he won't. He'll let us go."

"I'm just saying. You need to be ready to actually use that thing, if need be."

"I am. But I won't need to."

A clunking sound startled me awake. I was on the floor beside the bunk. I shot up. I never meant to fall asleep. Footsteps on the ladder. Isaac was back.

"Patti," I whispered.

She was leaning up against the wall. She'd fallen asleep too. She looked over at me, then realized what was going on.

"Fuck," she whispered.

A silhouette appeared at the end of the hallway. Isaac started moving toward us. I went to grab the shotgun, but Patti was already there. She picked it up and pointed it at the entrance.

"You two awake?" Isaac ducked into the room.

There was a blast. A flash of light. It felt like a bomb had gone off. I fell back against the wall. Patti fell into me. She'd pulled the trigger. She'd shot him. Dust and smoke filled the room.

Isaac was down on the ground. My ears rang. Patti was holding her arm and wincing. The shotgun lay on the ground in front of her.

I got up and moved over toward Isaac. He lay flat on his stomach. There was blood on the ground. He reached his hand out in front of him. Reaching for the gun. I kicked it toward the wall. Isaac lifted his head. Blood on his face. He looked up at me. I turned and positioned myself so that I was standing above Isaac, facing Patti, my feet straddling his shoulders. I reached down and grabbed the chain attached to my leg. There was just enough slack to wrap it around his throat. I started pulling at it.

Isaac struggled, but I put my foot on the back of his head. I pulled with all my strength, everything I had. Isaac thrashed and squirmed. I couldn't watch. I looked over at Patti. I couldn't hear her over the ringing in my ears, but I could see that she was screaming. I screamed, too. Dust everywhere. My ears still ringing. I pulled on the chain. Isaac struggled.

Then he stopped struggling. His body went limp beneath me. I kept pulling. And then I let go. It was over. I sat down on the ground beside Isaac's lifeless body and caught my breath.

34

I went through Isaac's pockets. I had to turn him over. His shirt was soaked with blood—it looked like Patti had got him in the ribs. I didn't dare look at his neck. There was a set of keys in one of his front pockets. I got Isaac's blood on my hands retrieving them. One of the keys was much smaller than the others. I tried it on the cuff around my ankle—it slipped right in. I removed the cuff and slid the keys over to Patti.

My ankle looked like one big blister. Sore as hell. I looked over at Patti. She was saying something to me, but I still couldn't hear over the ringing. The room smelled of sulphur.

"What?"

She pointed to the entrance. I took an unopened bottle of water from the floor and stepped over Isaac. Into the front room. Patti followed behind me, clutching her arm. I started up the ladder. I knew that the bunker door wouldn't be locked, because Isaac was down there with us, but I still braced myself for the horror of it not opening. I pushed open the door, which wasn't easy in my weakened state, and sunlight came pouring in. For some reason, I'd thought it was the middle of the night. I hadn't seen natural light in almost two weeks. I pulled myself up out of the hole and onto the grass. Patti emerged soon after. She only used one arm to climb the ladder—the recoil from the shotgun must have done something to the other one, I thought.

"Are you okay?"

"What?" Patti said.

I could hear her now. The ringing had died down a little. I stepped back over and closed the bunker door. I slid the latch shut. I then pulled the square carpet of grass over, hiding the door. I knew there was no reason to lock Isaac's dead body inside the bunker, but I had to do it. If I could've piled cement blocks on top of the door, I'd have done that too.

I opened my water bottle and drank half. Flies buzzing around me. The sun blazing above the trees. I passed the bottle to Patti and she swallowed the rest.

"Can you hear me now?"

"Yeah," she said. "Jesus Christ. What happened there?"

"Why did you shoot him?"

"I don't know. I was scared. It just happened. Why did you strangle him?"

"I was scared too. He was reaching for the gun."

"We killed him. You're covered in blood. I guess I am too. We're murderers now. Which way back to the road?"

I pointed west.

We walked in silence, the sun beating down on us. Moving slowly. Mosquitoes bit. My muscles ached and I wanted to lie down. I felt nauseous. Every time I stepped down with my right foot, which was the one that had been cuffed, a sharp pain shot up my leg. We didn't see anyone. Just birds and squirrels. We kept moving. It took us nearly an hour to reach the service road. Leonard's car was gone. Dougie's rental wasn't there, either. It would take us at least a half hour before we reached the first intersection, maybe longer. A vehicle might come along though, I thought, and we could hitch a ride to the police station. Borrow their phone. We started down the road.

"Listen," Patti said. "I'm coming back to Toronto. But I can't go home. No matter what happened to Dougie. Can I stay with you and your mom?"

"You want to live with me?"

"Just for a while. You can say no."

"I'd have to ask Mother. No, I don't need to ask her anything. She'd love to have you. Of course you can stay with me. You can even have my bed."

"I'm not taking your bed, Colleen."

"We'll see."

The intersection came into view. There weren't any vehicles in sight. We kept walking. The sun beating down on us. I stopped to throw up. It was just water. Patti helped me up and we continued. A truck appeared in the distance. It turned and started driving toward us. We stopped, waved our hands in the air. It slowed down but drove past us. A young woman in the driver's seat. She pulled over. Stuck her head out the window. It looked like she was wearing a Dairy Queen uniform.

"You two alright?" she said. "What happened?"

I opened my mouth to say something, but then just started crying. I couldn't help it. Somewhere in there, I collapsed.

I awoke in a hospital bed. No one else in the room. The curtains were closed, but I could tell that it was nighttime. I was hooked up to an IV. I could hear low voices in the hallway. My whole body ached. I called out for Patti, but no one answered. I soon fell back asleep.

The next time I opened my eyes, Mother was in the room. Sitting in a chair next to my bed. Staring down at the floor. She looked old. Having lived with her my whole life, I'd watched her age so gradually.

"Mother," I said.

She looked up. She'd been crying. She stood up tentatively, then rushed over to the bed and threw her arms around me. I cried out in pain.

"I'm sorry," Mother said. "You poor thing." But she kept hugging me.

I stayed in the hospital overnight. Mother too. She recounted how she'd become worried when I stopped answering her calls, until she eventually phoned the police and filed a Missing Person report. She'd barely slept since and had spent most of her time staring at her phone, waiting for updates that never came. It was like I'd vanished, she said. Leonard's car was still missing. In the morning, two detectives came in and interviewed me. I told them everything. Leonard, the trips to Niagara Falls, Isaac Kindler, the bunker. How Isaac and Woodbine were planning to revive the Citizens of Light, that they'd even purchased a new property. I asked them to check on a woman named Jess who worked at Roswell's restaurant in Niagara Falls, and make sure she was safe.

I was discharged later that day and Mother took me home. Patti was already there, with her stuff. She'd spent the previous afternoon in the hospital too but was sent home in the evening. She looked worn out, but she said she was fine.

"Any word on Dougie?" I stood in the entrance to Mother's room, where Patti sat on the bed with a bag of barbeque chips. Mother had decided to sleep on the couch so Patti could have her own space.

"They found his rental car," Patti said. "Stashed behind an abandoned strip mall outside of town. They found blood in the trunk."

"Oh no."

"They're going to test it, and they're obviously still looking. They'll call me. I just talked to Dougie's mom. They're all coming up here, staying at the house. This is so messed up."

"I'm sorry, Patti."

"Yeah, well I'm just glad to be above goddamn ground. Reporters have been coming around, by the way."

"Reporters?"

"I guess the story's already out. Did you talk to anyone?"

"Just the police."

"Get ready. I've been telling them all to piss off. But you do what you like."

Over the next few weeks, reporters did stop by the house. Phone calls came in. So many emails, from journalists and producers and podcasters. Police officers were stationed outside the house because of Isaac's connection to a criminal organization. I overheard a cashier at Shopper's Drug Mart talking about the story and learned that Woodbine had told an interviewer he had no knowledge of the bunker, or of Isaac's plans to break him out of prison. The cashier said that was baloney. I kept my head down. At Piccolos, I saw the Toronto *Metro* sitting out on a table and the front page had photos showing inside the bunker. I immediately returned home without buying anything. I did my best to ignore the media attention and focus on Patti and Mother. Make sure they were okay. In turn, they'd look out for me.

35

One evening, Mother made tea and grilled cheese sandwiches and we all sat together in the living room. A new *Riders of Exley* was about to start. Patti dipped her sandwich in her tea. She was using the blue Niagara Falls mug.

"The Niagara Falls mug," I said. "That's Leonard's, right?"

"Was it?" Mother said. "I thought we all kind of used it."

"I meant that Leonard bought it."

"Actually, I bought it. Is it upsetting you? I'll throw it out."

"No, it's fine. But when were you in Niagara Falls?"

"I wasn't. I found it at a yard sale."

"Why would you buy a mug that said Niagara Falls?"

"We needed a mug."

No one said anything for a while. We watched the show. Mother slurped her tea.

The episode began with Mary Valentine hearing ghostly voices coming out of the taps in the girls' washroom. The voices asked her to "come down here." Mary informed the headmaster, who told Mary to get more sleep and stop bothering her with such nonsense.

"That's the thing with this show," Patti said. "Every week something crazy happens with aliens or whatnot and the teachers never believe the kids. The writers ought to be shot."

"Actually, it could be part of a season-long arc," I said. "Where we find out the teachers are possessed by a supernatural force and so them not believing the kids is part of the world of the story."

"Or it could be the writers are a bunch of hacks."

"Give them some credit. I've seen some amazing episodes."

"How old is Mary Valentine supposed to be? She looks like she should be in college. Or graduated and working in an office."

"Brie Coolidge-Smith is twenty and the character is sixteen now, which isn't that far off. I think she looks quite young for her age actually."

"She looks like a grandma."

"Oh, stop it."

"And you can always tell it's a stunt person when the kids are on their horses. It's like they don't even try."

"Brie Coolidge-Smith does all her own riding."

"Who? Grandma?"

At this, Mother erupted with laughter. She dropped her sandwich. Convulsing with laughter, her body bent over.

"I'm sorry," Mother managed to get out. Her eyes were closed. She clutched at her ribs and shook with laughter. "I'm so sorry."

I started seeing a new therapist—Mother too. Patti said she'd think about going herself but wanted to wait and see how we "turned out." Dr. Brahn was nice, and her receptionist occasionally put out Danishes. What had happened in the bunker wouldn't leave my mind. I couldn't stop thinking about what I'd done to Isaac. The feeling of the chain around his neck, my foot pressed into the back of his head. Every time it passed through my mind, which was often, I automatically winced or let out a little moan. Dr. Brahn was helping me cope with all this. We talked about Leonard too. My grief. There was a lot to unpack, but Dr. Brahn made it all seem possible. That there was a way forward.

Patti returned to her old position at Innovative Business Standards. She said people were staring at her for the first few hours, but the novelty soon wore off and they all shifted focus back to their crosswords and crochet projects. Apparently, Ken got fired while we were gone. He caught this poor girl Tara playing Candy Crush while on a survey and he threw her phone so hard it went through the wall. I was reluctant to return to the call centre. I needed the money though. My chequing account was empty, and I'd maxed out my credit card in Niagara Falls. I owed Mother for the debt I racked up on her card too. I got in the car with Patti when she drove in for work one afternoon so I could ask about coming back. I waited downstairs while Patti went up—I didn't want to bother the supervisors during a shift change. I paced around the lobby for ten minutes and then stepped onto the elevator with two latecomers. Jimmy and Wanda. High school students, or they seemed young anyway. I'd worked with them for two years or so, though we'd never spoken. They didn't seem to recognize me.

"Do you think we'll get off early tonight?" Wanda asked.

"I don't know," Jimmy said. "We didn't get off early last night."

"I wouldn't mind if we got off an hour early tonight."

"Yeah. But then we lose one of our breaks."

"So? I'd rather get off an hour early than have the extra break."

"Yeah. But we'll get paid for the hour if we stay."

"True. I guess I'd like the extra hour's pay, but I'd also like to leave early."

"Yeah. I'm the same."

When Jimmy and Wanda got off at the call centre's floor, I stayed on and took the elevator back down to the lobby. I'd find something else.

Later in the week, Patti convinced me to go to The Blue Drop, the sports bar behind our house. I washed my face and we walked around the block to the front entrance. Even though I'd looked out onto The Blue Drop from my bedroom window since I was little kid, I'd never actually been inside. It wasn't so bad. From the parking lot, you get a different impression of the place. Like it was full of vomiting and public urination and curse words. But there were families eating burgers and people I recognized from Piccolos. Our mail carrier was at the bar, drinking a pint of beer with someone in a cowboy hat. The music was energetic but not too loud. Baskets of fries everywhere. No one bothered us. Patti and I sat in a booth near the washrooms. She ordered us each a vodka tonic.

"So," Patti said. "Two widows, out on the town."

"Patti," I said. "You don't know that Dougie's gone. He could be hiding somewhere. Just wait and see what the police find."

"He's dead. It's pretty clear. Which is obviously horrible, but whatever. Let's not talk about that."

"If that's what you want."

"You never told me about Leonard. What Isaac said. Do you know what happened?"

I told her what Isaac had told me, how he ordered Leonard to bring me out to the bunker. How Leonard, who was both entirely under Isaac's spell but still loyal to me, couldn't take the pressure.

"Leonard shot himself outside the bunker," I said. "There was no mysterious gunman. No Russian operative in the shadows. Just Leonard. He was struggling with something, all alone, and he couldn't take it anymore."

"That's horrible, Colleen," Patti said. "I'm sorry."

"Maybe I could have helped him. If he'd just talked to me."

"You didn't know."

"Exactly. I didn't know. My marriage was a joke. I didn't know my husband any more than I know the bartender over there."

"He's pretty cute, actually."

"I'm such an idiot. How could I not see that something was wrong?"

"You're not an idiot. Leonard hid all that stuff from you, and he was good at hiding it. He didn't want you to know about that side of him. And it's too bad you didn't know, I guess. But you can also think of it like you got to see the good parts of Leonard. He saved the best for you."

"I don't know about that."

"It's true. You know Ted Bundy? Well, there's the version of him that killed all those poor women. But he also worked at a suicide hotline. Do you know how many people he probably saved? He had a good side. It's like, if you were married to Ted Bundy and you only knew about the suicide hotline and you didn't know about all the murders. You wouldn't be married to the serial killer Ted Bundy. You'd be married to the Ted Bundy that helped people and saved lives."

"Leonard wasn't Ted Bundy," I said. "He didn't murder anyone."

"Even better," Patti said.

The comparison was off and a little offensive, but Patti had a point buried in there. The Leonard I knew was a good man. Kind. Loving, in his way. In hindsight, it wasn't the deepest, most meaningful relationship. We were like neighbours, or colleagues. But we got along. He made me happy. The good parts of our marriage were still good.

Patti and I drank more vodka tonics. We gossiped about the people from the call centre. We reminisced about Niagara Falls— the beginning, when things were still sort of fun. We were both pretty tipsy by the time we left the bar and we decided to hop the fence into Mother's backyard instead of walking around the block. I hoisted Patti up and she climbed over. I looked around on the ground for something to step on, like a bucket or recycling bin, and noticed a shiny object by my feet. I picked it up. Mother's harmonica.

Back home, the house was silent. Patti had gone to bed in Mother's room. Mother lay on the couch, drooling onto a throw pillow. I placed the harmonica on the coffee table so Mother would see it as soon as she woke up. I went to my room and opened the laptop. For the last time, I fired up *Reindeer Island*.

Heartsong ran through the moonlit parking lot. Past the tennis courts, up the bridal path, and finally out onto Lorenzo Snow Beach. He kept running. The expansive Golden Plates Hotel receded from view as Heartsong headed toward the north shore of the island.

Eventually Heartsong reached the spot I was looking for: Wilford Woodruff Cove. A small beach at the northernmost tip of the island. You had to pass through a stand of blinking Christmas trees to get to the cove, as it was hidden from view. A secret beach. In the exact centre of the cove, a small patch of land rose up out of the water. On this patch of land stood a golden statue of a reindeer with wings, ascending to the heavens. Heartsong walked to the middle of the beach and looked out at the statue, at the waves, and at the distant horizon, barely discernible under the dark sky. A gentle sea wind blowing through his fur. I left Heartsong standing on the beach and closed the laptop.

ACKNOWLEDGEMENTS

Katie Shelstad, Michael LaPointe, Clay Pearn, Kamil Chajder, Sam Haywood, Megan Philipp, Sheila Heti, Naben Ruthnum, Amy Jones, Terry Fallis, Tori Elliott, Taryn Boyd, Curtis Samuel, Kate Kennedy, Claire Philipson, Senica Maltese, Ingrid Paulson, Sydney Barnes.

Sam Shelstad is a regular contributor to *McSweeney's Internet Tendency* and his work has appeared in magazines including *The New Quarterly* and *Joyland*. He was longlisted for the CBC Short Story Prize, a runner up for the Thomas Morton Memorial Prize, and a finalist for a National Magazine Award. He is the author of the story collection *Cop House* (Nightwood Editions, 2017). Shelstad lives in Toronto. *Citizens of Light* is his first novel. You can find Sam online at samshelstad.com.